ISLINGTON

D0719594

Sam's hand was huge, tanned and broad, with long, skilled fingers that were capable of killing a man, bringing a baby back from the brink of death—and driving a woman out of her mind with pleasure.

The strength of it should have scared Cassidy, but for some strange reason it just felt…right. *He* felt right. As though her hand had been fashioned to fit perfectly into his.

But that was a dangerous illusion and one she needed to get out of her head. He wasn't perfect, she reminded herself firmly. He was fighting demons as hard as he fought for his country. The combination wasn't healthy. For either of them.

Dear Reader

My parents can attest to the fact that I was always a dreamer. At age eight I wanted to be a prima ballerina, but that didn't pan out because I also loved Westerns and ran around the garden with my brother shooting everything. Then I discovered Julie Andrews and wanted to be just like her. Well, as you can see, that didn't work out either, but my love of dreaming and weaving fantastical stories in my head finally did.

A few years ago a friend showed me an article in a magazine about a Mills & Boon® writing competition and urged me to enter. With absolutely nothing to lose, I did. I didn't win, but imagine my surprise and delight when I received an e-mail from the offices of Mills & Boon® Medical Romance™ saying they loved my writing style and absolutely adored my characters, Cassidy and Sam—*especially* Sam. It was a dream come true—or rather coming true.

It's been a hard slog getting Sam and Cassidy's story perfected, but with the infinitely patient Flo Nicoll and her expert advice it's done. and I'm *finally* able to say, 'I'm a published author.' What a thrill! Now my colleagues can stop saying, 'Why is this taking so long? Shouldn't you try something else?' And my daughters can stop rolling their eyes at me and admit I *am* Queen of the Universe—in our house anyway.

I really hope you enjoy reading about Sam and Cassidy's struggle to overcome their trust issues and admit they're perfect for each other. I also hope you enjoy your visit to Crescent Lake, with all its quirky characters. I've had such fun with them and hope you do too.

Happy reading!

Lucy

RESISTING HER REBEL HERO

BY
LUCY RYDER

Published in Great Britain 2014
by Mills & Boon, an imprint of Harlequin (UK) Limited,
Eton House, 18-24 Paradise Road, Richmond, Surrey, TW9 1SR

© 2014 Bev Riley

ISBN: 978 0 263 24213 3

Harlequin (UK) Limited's policy is to use papers that are natural, renewable and recyclable products and made from wood grown in sustainable forests. The logging and manufacturing processes conform to the legal environmental regulations of the country of origin.

Printed and bound in Great Britain
by CPI Antony Rowe, Chippenham, Wiltshire

After trying out everything from acting in musicals, singing opera, travelling and writing for a business newspaper, **Lucy Ryder** finally settled down to have a family and teach at a local community college, where she currently teaches English and Communication. However, she insists that writing is her first love and time spent on it is more pleasure than work.

She currently lives in South Africa, with her crazy dogs and two beautiful teenage daughters. When she's not driving her daughters around to their afternoon activities, cooking those endless meals or officiating at swim meets, she can be found tapping away at her keyboard, weaving her wild imagination into hot romantic scenes.

RESISTING HER REBEL HERO
is Lucy Ryder's debut title
for Harlequin Mills & Boon®!

DEDICATION

I couldn't have done this without my wonderful supportive family—especially my beautiful daughters, Caitlin and Ashleigh. I love you to infinity and beyond.

A special thanks to Dr Jenni Irvine, who started it all, and to Flo Nicoll for seeing something in my writing she liked.

And lastly to my colleagues—ladies, it's amazing how people bond through complaining.

CHAPTER ONE

THE LAST PLACE Dr. Cassidy Mahoney expected to find herself when she fled the city for a wilderness town deep in the
Cascades Mountains was the county jail. She could hon-
estly say it was the first time she'd ever been in one, and
with the smell of stale alcohol and something more basi-
cally human permeating the air, she hoped it was the last.

And absolutely nothing could have prepared her for
him—all six feet four inches of broad shoulders and hard
muscles, oozing enough testosterone to choke a roomful
of hardened feminists.

Draped languorously over a narrow bunk that clearly
couldn't contain his wide shoulders and long legs, the man
lustily sang about a pretty *señorita* with dark flashing eyes
and lips like wine. The old man in the neighboring cell
cheerfully sang along, sounding like a rusty engine chug-
ging up a mountain pass while his cellmate snored loudly
enough to rattle the small windows set high in the outside wall.

Pausing in the outer doorway, Cassidy felt her eyes
widen and wondered if she'd stepped onto a movie set without a script. The entire town of Crescent Lake had turned
out to be like something from a movie set and she was still
having a hard time believing she wasn't dreaming.

Quite frankly, even her wildest dreams couldn't have
conjured up being escorted to the sheriff's office in a police

cruiser like a seasoned offender—even to supply medical care to a prisoner.

From somewhere near the back of the holding area a loud voice cursed loudly and yelled at them to "shut the hell up." Hazel Porter, the tiny woman currently leading Cassidy into the unknown, pushed the door open all the way and gestured for her to follow.

"Full house tonight," Hazel rasped in her thirty-a-day voice, sounding like she'd been sucking on smokes since the cradle. "Must be full moon." She nodded to the cell holding the old-timers. "Don't mind them, honey: long-standing weekend reservations." Her bunch of keys jangled Cassidy's already ragged nerves.

"And ignore the guy in the back," Hazel advised. "Been snarlin' and snipin' since he was hauled in a couple hours ago. I was tempted to call in animal control, but the sheriff said to let him sleep it off."

"I'd be sleeping too, you old crow, if it wasn't for the caterwauling, stripping paint off the walls."

Hazel shook her head. "Mean as a cornered badger, that one," she snorted, closing the outer door behind them. "Even when he ain't drunk."

Cassidy sent the woman a wary look, a bit nervous at the thought of being closed in with a bunch of offenders—one of whom was apparently violent—and a pint-sized deputy who could be anything between sixty and a hundred and sixty.

"So…the patient?" she prompted uncertainly, hoping it wasn't the fun guy in back. Hippocratic oath aside, she drew the line at entering his cell without the sheriff, a couple of burly deputies and a fully charged stun gun as backup.

"That'll be Crescent Lake's very own superhero." Hazel headed for the baritone's cell and Cassidy couldn't help the relief that left her knees a bit shaky. "He's a recent addition and a wild one, so watch yerself," wasn't exactly something Cassidy wanted to hear.

The deputy slid a key into the lock and continued as though she'd known Cassidy for years. "Wasn't a bit surprising when he up 'n left med school to join the Navy." Her chuckle sounded like a raspy snort. "Heck, 'Born to be wild' shoulda been tattooed on that boy's hide at birth."

Cassidy blinked, unsure if she was meant to respond and uncertain what she would say if she did. She'd learnt over the past fortnight that mountain folk were for the most part polite and taciturn with strangers, but treated everyone's business like public property. She'd even overheard bets being placed on how long *she'd* last before she "hightailed it back to the city."

The sound of the key turning was unnaturally loud and Cassidy bit her lip nervously when the cell door slid open and clanged against the bars. Drawing in a shaky breath, she smoothed damp palms down her thighs and eyed the "born to be wild" man warily.

One long leg was bent at the knee; the other hung over the side of the bunk, large booted foot planted on the bare concrete floor. Although a bent arm blocked most of his face from view, Cassidy realized she was the object of intense scrutiny. Her first thought was, *God, he's huge,* followed almost immediately by, *And there's only a garden gnome's granny between me and Goliath's drunk younger brother.*

"Is that why he's in here?"

"Heck, no," Hazel rasped with a snort. "Was the only way Sheriff could be sure he stayed put till you arrived. Boy thinks he's too tough for a few stitches and a couple of sticking plasters."

Cassidy hovered outside the cell, aware that her heart was banging against her ribs like she was the one who'd committed a felony and was facing jail time. Besides, she'd heard all about people going missing in wilderness towns and had the oddest feeling the instant she stepped over the threshold her life would never be the same.

Turning, she caught the older woman watching her and gave a self-conscious shrug. "Is it safe? Shouldn't we wait for the sheriff? A couple of deputies?" A shock stick?

Small brown eyes twinkled. "Safe?" Hazel cackled as though the idea tickled her funny bone when Cassidy had been as serious as a tax audit. In Boston, violent offenders were always accompanied by several burly cops, even when they were restrained.

"Well, now," the deputy said, wiping the mirth from her eyes. "I don't know as the boy's ever been called 'safe' before, but if you're wondering if he'll get violent, don't you worry about a thing, hon. He's gentle as a lamb."

Cassidy's gaze slid to the "boy," who seemed to be all shoulders and legs, and thought, *Yeah, right.* Nothing about him looked gentle and "boy" wasn't something he'd been for a good long time. Not with that long, hard body or the toxic cloud of testosterone and pheromones filling the small space and snaking primitive warnings up her spine.

Even sprawled across the narrow bunk, he exuded enough masculine sexuality to have a cautious woman taking a hasty step in retreat.

Hazel Porter must have correctly interpreted the move for she cackled gleefully even as she planted a bony hand in the small of Cassidy's back and gave her a not-so-gentle shove into the cell.

Her pulse gave an alarmed little blip and Cassidy found herself swallowing a distressed yelp, which was ridiculous, considering he'd done nothing more dangerous than sing in that rich, smooth bedroom baritone.

"Whatcha got for me, sweetheart?" the deep voice drawled, sending a shiver of fear down Cassidy's spine. At least she thought the belly-clenching, free-falling sensation was fear as goose bumps rushed over her skin beneath the baby-pink scrubs top she hadn't had time to change out of. The baby-pink top that was covered in little bear doctors and nurses and an assortment of smears and stains from a day spent with babies and toddlers.

Not exactly the kind of outfit that gave a woman much-needed confidence when facing a large alpha male.

"You get the rare steak and fries I ordered?"

Hazel snorted. "We're not running some five-star establishment here, sonny," she rebuked mildly, eyeing him over her spectacles. "You wanted steak and fries you shoulda thought about that *before* you decided to pound on Wes."

A battered lip curved into a loopy grin. "Aw, c'mon, Hazel." He chuckled, sounding a little rusty, as though he hadn't had much to laugh about lately—or had awakened from a deep sleep. "He was drunker than a sailor on shore leave. The coeds he was hassling were terrified. 'Sides, *someone* had to stop him trashing Hannah's bar. He threw a *stool* at her when she tried to intervene, for God's sake."

"Your sister can handle herself," Hazel pointed out reasonably, to which the hunk sleepily replied, "Sure she can. We taught her some great moves." He yawned until his jaw cracked. "Jus' doin' my brotherly duty, 'sall."

"And look where that got you."

The man lifted a hand wrapped in a bloodied bar towel and peered down at his side. "Bonehead took me by surprise," he growled in disgust, wincing as he lowered his arm. "Was on me before I could convince them to leave." He grunted. "Better my hide than her pretty face, huh?"

"You're a good brother," Hazel said dryly.

A wide shoulder hitched. "Didn't you teach me to stand up to the bullies of this world, ma'am?"

"*Ri-ight.*" Hazel snorted, beaming at him with affectionate pride. "Blame the helpless old lady."

The deep chuckle filling the tiny cell did odd things to Cassidy's insides and spread prickling warmth throughout her body. Her face heated and the backs of her knees tingled.

She uttered a tiny gasp.

Tingled? Really? Alarmed by her body's response, she backed up a step until she realized what she was doing and froze. Feeling her face heat, Cassidy drew in a shaky breath and took a determined step forward. She dropped her medical bag between his long hard thighs since he took up the rest of the bunk.

So what if she was dressed like a kindergarten teacher? She was a mature, professional woman who'd spent an entire day with babies and toddlers—not some silly naïve schoolgirl dazzled by a pair of wide shoulders, long legs and a deep bedroom voice.

Well…not usually. Besides, she'd already done that and was not going there again. *Tingling* of any sort. Was out.

"Nothin' helpless about you, darlin'," the bedroom voice drawled with another flash of even white teeth as Cassidy pulled out a pair of surgical gloves. She couldn't see his eyes but knew by the stillness of his body that he was tracking her every move.

"Save the sweet talk, sonny," Hazel sniffed, amused yet clearly not taken in by the charm. "And play nice. Miz Mahoney doesn't have time to waste on idiots."

Cassidy snapped on a latex glove and opened her mouth to correct the deputy's use of "Miz" but he shifted at that moment and every thought fled, leaving her numb with shock as she realized exactly who she was in a jail cell with.

Ohmigosh. Her eyes widened. *He really was a superhero.* Or rather Major Samuel J. Kellan, Crescent Lake's infamous Navy SEAL and all-round bad boy. She stared at him and wondered if she was hallucinating. Wasn't he supposed to be a local hero or something? Heck, a *national* hero?

What was he doing in the county jail?

Besides, he'd been injured protecting his sister and saving a couple of young women from harm. And according to local gossip, everyone adored him. Women swooned at the mention of his name and men tended to recount his exploits like he was some kind of legendary superhero. And *really*. There wasn't a man alive who could do *half* the things Major Kellan was rumored to have done and survived. Well…*not* outside Hollywood.

Yet, even battered and bruised, it was clear the man deserved his reputation as big, bad and dangerous to know. Looking into his battered face, it was just as clear that one thing *hadn't* been exaggerated. With his thick dark hair, fierce gold eyes, strong shadowed jaw and surprisingly sensual mouth, the man *was* as hot as women claimed. She could only be grateful she'd been immunized against fallen angels masquerading as wounded bad boys.

Frankly, the *last* thing she needed in her life was another man with more sex appeal than conscience. Heck, the last thing she needed, *period*, was a man—especially one who tended to suck the air right out of a room and make the backs of her knees sweat.

Hazel cleared her throat loudly, jolting Cassidy from her bizarre thoughts. "Anything you need before you sew up his pretty face, hon?"

"He really should be taken to the hospital," Cassidy said briskly, ignoring the strong smell of hops and thickly lashed eyes watching her every move. "I'll need a lot more supplies than I have with me. Supplies I can only get at the hospital." Especially if the hand wound was serious. Nerve damage was notoriously tricky to repair.

"Not to worry," Hazel rasped cheerfully. "Sheriff keeps all kinds of stuff ready for when the doc's called in unexpectedly. I'll pull Larry off front desk and send him in. You'll have your ER in a jiffy." And before Cassidy could tell the woman a jail cell was hardly a sterile environment, the desk sergeant disappeared, leaving her standing there gaping at empty space and wondering if she'd taken a left turn somewhere into an alternate universe where pint-sized deputies left unsuspecting young doctors alone in jail cells with a violent offender and…and *him*.

Her heart jerked hard against her ribs and a prickle of alarm eased up her spine. The closest thing she had to a weapon was a syringe and, frankly, even tanked, her patient looked like he could disarm her with a flick of one long-fingered hand.

Frowning, she slid a cautious look over her shoulder, trying to decide if she should make a break for it, when his voice enfolded her like rich, sinful chocolate. It took her a moment to realize that she had bigger problems.

"Hey, darlin'," he drawled, "wha's a nice girl like you doin' in a place like this?"

You have got to be kidding me.

Ignoring the lazy smile full of lethal charm, Cassidy sent him a sharp assessing look and wondered if his head injury was worse than it appeared. According to gossip, Major Hotstuff—her staff's name for him, not hers—was smooth as hundred-year-old bourbon and just as potent. *That* line had been about as smooth as a nerd in a room full of cheerleaders.

Opening her mouth to tell him that she'd heard more original pickup lines from paralytic drunks and whacked-out druggies, Cassidy's gaze locked with his and she was abruptly sucked into molten eyes filled with humor and sharp intelligence. Whether it was a trick of the light or the leashed power in his big, hard body, she was left with the weirdest impression that he wasn't nearly as drunk as he seemed, which was darned confusing, since he smelled like a brewery on a hot day.

This close she could clearly make out the dark ring encircling those unusual irises, and with the light striking his eyes from the overhead fixture, the tiny amber flecks scattered in the topaz made them appear almost gold. Like a sleek, silent jaguar.

A frisson of primitive awareness raced over her skin

and she tore her gaze from his, thinking, *Get a grip, Cassidy. He's the pied piper of female hormones. He seduces women to pass the time, for heaven's sake. And we are so done with that, remember?* Unfortunately, the appalling truth was that *her* hormones, frozen for far too long, had chosen the worst possible moment to awaken.

Annoyed and a little spooked, she drew her brows together and reached for his hand, abruptly all business. She was here to do a job, she reminded herself sharply, not get her hormones overhauled.

But the instant their skin touched, a jolt of electricity zinged up her arm to her elbow.

She yanked at her hand and stumbled back a step. Her head went light, her knees wobbled and she felt like she'd just been zapped by a thousand volts of live current. He must have felt it too because he grunted and looked startled, leaving Cassidy struggling with the urge to check if her hair was on fire.

Realizing her mouth was hanging open, she snapped it closed and reminded herself this was just another example of static electricity. *Big deal. Absolutely nothing to get excited about. Happens all the time.*

However, one look out the corner of her eye made her question whether the thin mountain air was killing off brain cells because Crescent Lake's hotshot hero could hardly be termed "just another" *anything*. With his thick, nearly black hair mussed around his head like a dark halo, glowing gold eyes and fallen-angel looks, he was about as ordinary as a tiger shark in a goldfish bowl.

Giving her head a shake, Cassidy realized she was getting a little hysterical and probably looked like an idiot standing there gaping at him like he'd grown horns and a tail.

Exhaling in a rush, she looked around for the missing glove. And spied it on the bunk.

Right between his hard jeans-clad thighs.

Her body went hot and her mouth went dry because, *holy Toledo*, those jeans fit him like they'd been molded to...well, *everything*.

Tearing her gaze away from checking out places she had no business checking out, she reached for the latex glove and gasped when their hands collided. He picked up the glove and held it out, tightening his grip when she reached for it. Her automatic "Thank you" froze in her throat when she looked up and caught his sleepy gaze locked on her... mouth. After a long moment his eyes rose.

Cassidy's pulse took off like a sprinter off the starting blocks and all she could think was... *No! Oh, no. Not happening, Cassidy. Get your mind on the job.*

Her brow wrinkling with irritation, she tugged and told herself she was probably just light-headed from all the fresh mountain air. Dr. Mahoney did *not* flutter just because some bad boy looked at her with his sexy eyes or talked in a rough baritone that she felt all the way to her belly.

"Excuse me?" she said in a tone that was cool and barely polite.

"I don't bite," he slurred with a loopy grin. "Unless you ask real nice."

Narrowing her gaze, she yanked the glove free and considered smacking him with it. She was not there to play games with some hotshot Navy SEAL, thank you very much.

Setting her jaw, she wrestled with the glove a moment then reached for his hand when she was suitably protected.

"So..." he drawled after a long silence, during which she removed the blood-soaked bar towels to examine his injury, "where's the cute white outfit?"

She looked up to catch him frowning at her pink scrubs top and jeans. "White outfit?"

"Yeah. You know...white, short, lots of little buttons?" He leaned sideways to scan the empty cell. "And where's the box?"

"Box?" *What the heck was he talking about?*

"The boom box," he said, as though she was missing a few IQ points. "Can't dance without music."

What?

"I am not a stripper, Major Kellan," she said coolly, barely resisting the urge to grind her teeth. "And nurses don't wear those any more." She was accustomed to being mistaken for a nurse and on occasion an angel. But a stripper was a new one and she didn't know whether to laugh or stab him with her syringe. Instead, she lifted a hand to brush a thick lock of dark hair off his forehead to check his head wound. He had to be hemorrhaging in there somewhere to have mistaken her for a stripper. Her hair was pulled back in a messy ponytail and her makeup had worn off hours ago.

So not stripper material.

"You're not?" He sounded disappointed. She ignored him. The wound only needed a few butterfly strips and he'd probably have a whopping headache on top of a hangover. *Hmph. That's what you get for making a woman flutter without her permission, hotshot.*

His left eye was almost swollen shut and a bruise had already turned the skin around it a dark mottled red. She gently probed the area and found no shifting under the skin. No cracked bones, but he'd have a beaut of a shiner and his split lip looked painful enough to put a crimp in his social life.

No kissing in his *immediate future.*

Wondering where that thought had come from, Cassidy reached into the bag for packaged alcohol swabs. "He did a good job on your face," she murmured, dabbing at the wound.

Something lethal came and went in his expression, too quickly for Cassidy to interpret. But when he smirked and said, "You should see the other guys," she decided she must have been mistaken and finally gave in to the mental eye roll that had been threatening. Other *guys*?

Maybe he'd been listening to too many stories about his own exploits.

"And I guess the knife wasn't clean either?"

He grunted, but as she wasn't fluent in manspeak, she was unsure if he was agreeing with her or in pain. "Broken beer bottle. Talk about a cliché," he snorted roughly. "And forget the tetanus shot. Had one a few months ago… so I'm good."

Good? It was her turn to snort—silently, of course.

Her obvious skepticism prompted an exasperated grimace. "I'm not drunk."

She eyed him suspiciously. "You're not?"

He shook his head and yawned again. "Just tired. An' it's Friday," he reminded her as though she should know what he was talking about.

"Been carousing it up with the boys, have you?"

His look was reproachful. "Fridays are busy and Hannah's usual bartender has food poisoning."

"So, you were what?" Cassidy inquired dryly. "Keeping the peace as you served up whiskey and bar nuts?"

His gold eyes gleamed with appreciation and his battered lip curved in a lopsided smile. "If you're worried, you could always stay the night. Just to be sure I'm not suffering from anything…fatal."

Flicking on a penlight, Cassidy leaned closer. "I'm sure that won't be necessary, Major," she responded dryly, checking his pupil reaction. The only fatal thing *he* was suffering from was testosterone overload.

She stepped back to pick up another alcohol swab, before returning to press it to the bloodied cut above his eye. His hissed reaction had her gentling her touch as she cleaned it. "How much did you have to drink?"

"A couple," he murmured, then responded to her narrow-eyed survey with a cocky smile that looked far too harmless for a man with his reputation. "Of sodas," he added innocently, and her assessing look turned speculative. For a man who slurred like a drunk and smelled as though he'd bathed in beer, his gaze was surprisingly sharp and clear.

"I don't drink on the job," he said, hooking a finger in the hem of her top, and giving a little tug. His knuckles brushed against bare skin and sent goose bumps chasing across her skin. "Beer and stupidity don't mix well."

"Mmm," she hummed, straight-faced, turning away to hide her body's reaction to that casual touch. "Do you need help removing your shirt?" she asked over her shoulder as she cleared away the soiled swabs. "I want to see your torso."

He was silent for a few beats and when the air thickened, she lifted her gaze and her breath caught. "Your…um… torso wound, I mean." It was no wonder he had women swooning all over the county.

As though reading her thoughts, his lips curled, drawing her reluctant gaze. The poet's mouth and long inky lashes should have looked ridiculously feminine on a man so blatantly male but they only made him appear harder, more masculine somehow.

"Isn't that supposed to be my line?"

Cursing the fair complexion that heated beneath his wicked gaze, Cassidy injected a little more frost into her tone. "Excuse me?"

His grin widened and he let out a rusty chuckle. "I like the way you say that. All cool and snooty and just a little bit superior."

Leveling him with a look one generally reserved for ill-mannered adolescents, Cassidy queried mildly, "Are you flirting with me, Major Kellan?"

"Me?" Then he chuckled. "If you have to ask," he drawled, leaning so close that she found herself retreating in an attempt to evade his potent masculine scent, "then I guess I'm out of practice."

She said, "Uh huh," and reached for the hem of his torn, bloodied T-shirt, pulling it from his waistband. The soft cotton was warm from his body and reeked of beer and something intrinsically male. She hastily drew it over his head and dropped it onto the bunk, ignoring his finely sculpted warrior's body. It had been a long time since she'd found herself this close to a man who made her want to bury her nose in his throat and breathe in warm manly skin.

But medical professionals didn't go around sniffing people's necks or drooling over every set of spectacular biceps, triceps or awesome abs that ended up in their ER. And they certainly didn't get the urge to follow that silky-looking happy trail that disappeared into a low-riding waistband with their lips either.

Or they shouldn't, she lectured herself sternly, considering the last one had left her with a deep sense of betrayal and a determination not to get sucked in again by a set of hard abs and a wicked smile.

Relieved to focus on something other than silky hair and warm manly skin, she leaned closer to probe the wound, murmuring an apology when he gave a sharp hiss. Over three inches long, it angled upwards towards his pec and the surrounding area was already darkening into what looked like the shape of a fist. Wincing, she ran the tips of her fingers over the bruised area just as the outer door banged opened, slamming against the wall.

The sound was as loud and unexpected as a gunshot. In a blur of eerily silent movement, Major Kellan surged off the bunk, shoving her roughly aside as he dropped into a crouch. Deadly menace slashed the air, sending Cassidy stumbling backwards.

She gave a shocked gasp and gaped at a wide, perfectly proportioned, perfectly tanned, muscular back bare inches from her face.

CHAPTER TWO

INSTANTLY ALERT AND battle-ready, Sam barely felt the burn of his injured palm or the line of fire streaking across his belly. Adrenaline and blood stormed his system and in some distant corner of his brain he realized it was happening. Again. *Dammit.*

Not now. Please, not now.

But he was helpless to stop it—helpless against the firestorm of images that tended to explode in his brain—instantly warping his sense of reality and triggering an instinct to protect. With deadly force.

From somewhere behind him he heard a gasp, and the young deputy entering the holding area abruptly stopped in his tracks.

One look at Sam and the kid's eyes widened to dinner plates. He went sheet-white and dropped the fold-up steel table. It teetered a moment then toppled over with loud clatter. The deputy jerked back as though he'd been prodded with a shock stick.

"M-Major K-Kellan?" he squeaked, his wide-eyed look of terrified embarrassment reaching Sam as though from a distance.

"It's just m-me, M-Major Kellan. L-Larry?"

Pain lanced through Sam's skull and he staggered, clutching his head. Sweat broke out along his spine so abruptly he felt dizzy. His strength drained, along with the surge of adrenaline that had fired his synapses and instinctively turned him into a lethal weapon. It had also turned him into something he didn't recognize any more. Something he didn't like.

Sam forced back the bile that came with particularly bad flashbacks—triggered no doubt by the violence of the evening and the sudden unexpected noise. *Dammit*. He wanted to smash his fist into the wall and roar with anger and despair.

But he couldn't…*couldn't* lose control now. Not with an audience.

The blood drained abruptly from his head, leaving him clammy and light-headed. "Dammit, Larry," he growled, and sagged as though someone had cut him off at the knees.

Squeezing his eyes closed to block out the wildly spinning cell, he staggered and hoped he wouldn't embarrass himself by passing out—or tossing his cookies. He could just imagine what the sexy nurse would think about the hotshot SEAL then.

"I'm s-sorry, M-Major…it's just that I had b-both hands f-full."

He felt her an instant before her arms wrapped around him, easing him backwards, soft and silky and smelling like cool mountain air. Mortified, Sam pulled away and collapsed wearily onto the narrow bunk, slinging an arm across his face.

"Don' sweat it, kid," he slurred, and prayed for oblivion. Unfortunately, sleep always came with a heavy price and he wasn't ready to go there. The nightmares were still too real, the memories too raw, the latest flashback still too recent. So vivid he could taste the fear, hear the furious pounding of his pulse in his head.

The Navy shrinks had warned that they'd get worse before they got better. They'd also warned that they'd last for years.

Well, hell. Just what he was looking forward to. A constant reminder of his greatest failure.

"Major Kellan?"

In the meantime he had to face Nurse…what's-her-name.

Swiping his good hand over his face, he eased open his eyes and focused on the statuesque blonde watching him warily and with more than a hint of concern.

He didn't want her pity—or anything else she had to offer. He wanted to be left alone. *Needed* to be left alone. "I'm fine," he snapped, furious with himself and embarrassed that she'd witnessed an episode. Hoping to distract his brain from the endless loop of horrifying images, Sam focused his attention on her.

Yeah, much better to focus on the nurse.

With her thick silvery blond hair haphazardly pulled off a stunning face dominated by deep green eyes and a lush wide mouth, she looked like a sexy angel and smelled like a wood sprite—all fresh and clean and earthy like the mountains in spring. Raindrops glistened in her hair like diamonds, giving her an ethereal quality that made him wonder if he *was* drunk or just plain losing it.

"No, you're not," she contradicted softly. "But you will be."

For one confused moment Sam wondered if he'd spoken his thoughts out loud before he remembered he'd said he was fine.

"Sure," he growled, clenching his teeth on a wave of grief and anger. I *will. But my friends are still dead. And the woman patching me up thinks Crescent Lake's hero is a whacked-out crazy with a drinking problem.*

Yeah, right. Hero. What a joke.

Heroes didn't let their teams down. They didn't return home with their buddies in body bags no matter what the Navy shrinks said. But his week of detention in a small, dark hole, deep in mountainous enemy territory wasn't something he talked about. He could barely *think* about it let alone talk about the hours of interrogation and torture that had left half his team dead.

The only reason *he'd* survived long enough to escape had been because they'd found out he was a medic and wanted him to treat some sick kid. He'd tried to bargain until they let his team go but they'd dragged in the team rookie and held a gun to his head. Afterwards they'd—

No. Don't go there. Not when the horror was still so fresh in his mind that every time he closed his eyes, he was back in that hellhole.

"Major Kellan?"

Jolted from his unpleasant thoughts, Sam saw the syringe and shot out his hand to wrap hard fingers around her wrist. Other than a slight widening of her eyes, the nurse held her ground without flinching. After a couple of tense beats she arched her brow, the move managing to convey a boatload of indulgent concern. Like he was a cranky toddler up past his bedtime. He groaned silently. *Just great.*

His face heated and he narrowed his eyes but she silently held his gaze, like he wasn't almost a foot taller, a hundred pounds heavier, and a whole hell of a lot meaner.

Clearly the woman was missing a few IQ points, he decided with a mix of admiration and annoyance, or she wasn't as soft and silky as she looked. He closed his eyes on a surge of self-disgust. All he needed to complete his humiliation was for her to ruffle his hair and kiss his "owie" better.

Way to go, hotshot.

"Do I need to wave a white flag or are you a friendly?" she asked with a hint of amusement, and when his lashes rose, she indicated the hand wrapped around her wrist.

He grimaced and released her. *Jeez, could this get any worse?* Embarrassment had him muttering, "I don't hit women." He jerked his chin at the syringe. "Unless they're armed."

She followed his gaze. "Oh, this?" Her mouth curved

sweetly into a smile that instantly made him suspicious *and* want to take a greedy bite of that lush lower lip. "Surely you're not afraid of a little needle, Major?" Her smile grew as though she'd just learnt his deepest, darkest secret. *Not even close, lady.* "A big tough SEAL like you?" She made a soothing sound in the back of her throat. "It won't hurt a bit. Trust me."

Sam grunted out a laugh and hauled himself into a sitting position, hissing through clenched teeth when the move sent pain radiating through his chest and burning across his belly. "That's what they all say," he growled. "Right before they stab you in the heart."

"Not to worry," she said, moving closer and wrapping him in clean mountain air. "I have no interest in your heart, Major. I'm aiming a little lower than that."

And then, as though suddenly realizing what she'd said, her cheeks turned pink and she sucked in a sharp breath while Sam choked out a stunned "*Huh?*" and dropped his uninjured hand to protect his crotch.

"Not th-that low," she stuttered with a strangled snicker. "Although I'd probably be doing the rest of the female population a favor."

He choked for the second time in as many seconds but before he could demand what she meant, the outer door banged open again and she froze, eyes jerking to his, all wide and apprehensive as though she expected him to go all psycho GI Joe on her.

Dammit. He did not go around terrorizing women. Well…not unless they were holding a machine gun on him. Then all bets were off.

Scowling, he opened his mouth to tell her to knock it off, but his brother strode into the holding cells looking all officious and in charge, and Sam turned his irritation on someone more deserving.

Unfortunately, one look at Ruben's face had Sam's annoyance abruptly fading. He knew that look. Had seen it a thousand times on his CO's face. Something was up. Something bad.

"I hope you haven't used that on him yet." Ruben tossed an armful of clothing onto the bunk. "Get dressed," he told Sam. "We're heading out."

Blondie gasped and stepped between them. "What—? No!" she hissed. "Are you insane?"

Sam ignored her outburst and rose, pain abruptly receding as his SEAL training took over. "What happened?"

"A group of hikers didn't check in after closing," Ruben said, his wary gaze flicking to the syringe, "and the weather's turned bad. Park rangers just found their vehicle up near Pike's Pass. Lake route turned up empty and they think the group took the trail leading up into the mountains."

"Elk Ridge," Sam guessed, fatigue instantly forgotten as adrenaline surged through his veins. Here was the opportunity he hadn't even realized he'd been waiting for, to get out there and do something more useful than working the taps at his sister's bar. Frankly, after months of "recuperation" he was thoroughly sick of his own company and damn tired of sitting around feeling sorry for himself.

Ruben nodded and backed away, keeping a wary eye on Cassidy, as though expecting her to use the syringe on *him*. "Can't you just wrap him up or something? My usual tracker had a family emergency and we're in a hurry."

Her eyes widened. "Wrap—? He's not a cheeseburger," she snapped, sending Ruben's eyebrows into his hairline. "And in case it escaped your notice, Sheriff, the major is bleeding, *and* he's been drinking. It would be suicidal to go climbing mountains in his condition. I'm going to insist you leave him here. Or, better yet, let me take him to the hospital."

Sam brushed past her to where Larry had set out the medical supplies. "I'm fine," he said brusquely, reaching for a wound dressing. "I told you I wasn't drunk."

Before he could open the packet she snatched it from him and shoved her shoulder into his side as though she'd physically keep him from leaving.

As if.

He would have snickered at the absurdity if he hadn't been sucking in a painful breath. Turning a scowl on her that usually had people backing off in a hurry, she surprised him with a snapped "Back it up, Major," clearly not intimidated by his big bad Navy SEAL attitude.

He gave an annoyed grunt and tried to snatch it back.

"I mean it," she warned, jabbing her finger into his chest. "Or I'll use the syringe and the sheriff will have no choice but to go without you." She narrowed her eyes at him when he continued to glare at her while contemplating letting her try.

Heck, he might even enjoy it.

"And FYI, *buddy*, I nearly got intoxicated on the alcoholic haze surrounding you when I arrived, and not five minutes ago you almost fell on your face. You are *not* in any condition to go anywhere, least of all into the mountains on S&R. Besides," she reasoned sweetly, "you're bleeding all over the sheriff's nice clean jail cell. You need stitches." She paused and dropped her eyes meaningfully to his hand and then his abdomen. "Lots of them."

Staring down at her, Sam felt his lips twitch. She was like an enraged kitten—all fierce green eyes and ruffled silver fur. For just an instant he was tempted to reach out and smooth his hands over all that soft skin and silky silvery blond hair until she purred. One look into her narrowed eyes, however, and Sam knew she would probably bite his hand off at the wrist if he tried.

He made a scoffing sound filled with masculine impatience and amusement, which only served to narrow her eyes even further. "I've had mosquito bites worse than this," he assured her, feeling unaccountably cheered by her concern. "And if you're worried about blood alcohol levels, I'm sure the sheriff can organize a breathalyzer."

For long tense moments they engaged in a silent battle of wills until she finally uttered a soft "*Aargh*" followed by "Fine" in a tone that clearly meant it wasn't, and Sam had to clench his teeth to keep from grinning. He had a feeling grinning would be bad for his health.

"Oh…and FYI, *sweetheart*," he continued, while she sorted through the supplies with barely leashed temper, "I wasn't drinking. The weasel tried to break a bottle over my head. When I ducked, it shattered against the bar and soaked into my shirt. That was *before* he tried to gut me with it."

She turned towards him with a derisive sound and raised a brow that clearly conveyed her opinion of his explanation. "I said fine, didn't I?"

"You most certainly did," Ruben said dryly, shoving his face between them. "But I'm still not seeing anything happening here, people." He waited a couple of beats as his gaze ping-ponged between them. "So if you kids could save the lovers' spat for another time, I'd like my chief tracker."

Feeling her face catch fire, Cassidy broke eye contact with the Navy SEAL to send the sheriff a long, silent, narrow-eyed look that had him backing away with his hands up.

She turned back to snap, "Lift your arm." When he did she swiped disinfectant across the angry gash, completely ignoring the hissed response to her cavalier treatment.

After a long murmured conversation during which she cleaned and applied a few adhesive cross-strips to keep the edges of the wound together, the sheriff left. Cassidy knew the instant the SEAL's attention shifted back to her because the tiny hairs on the back of her neck prickled.

With unsteady hands she dressed his wound then cleaned and tightly wrapped his hand in a waterproof dressing, before turning away to gather the debris.

The length of her back heated an instant before a long tanned arm reached over her shoulder to snag a bandage. Cursing the way her skin prickled and her body tightened with some kind of weird anticipation, she sent a dark look over her shoulder and watched in silence as he awkwardly attempted to wrap it around his torso. After a moment she sighed and put out her hand, saying wearily, "I'll do it."

Clearly surprised by her offer, Samuel held her gaze for a long tension-filled moment. His laugh was a husky rasp in the tense silence and did annoying things to her breathing. "You're not going to strangle me with it, are you?"

Cassidy knew the taping would help him move—and breathe—more comfortably as he leapt tall mountains in a single bound. She rolled her eyes and waited while he gingerly raised his arms to link both hands behind his head.

Hard muscles shifted beneath his taut, tanned skin and she had to bite her lip to keep from sighing like a stupid female drunk on manly pheromones. She swallowed the urge to lean forward and swipe her tongue across his strong, tanned throat. As though he'd read her mind, he sucked in a sharp breath and she froze, watching in awed fascination as flesh rippled and goose bumps broke out across his skin an inch from her nose.

Heat snapped in the air between them and her mind went numb. *Good grief,* she thought with horror, *I'm attracted to him?* Appalled and more than a little rattled, she lifted her gaze, only to find him watching her, the expression in his gold eyes sending her blood pressure shooting into the stratosphere. She didn't have to wonder if he was as affected by their proximity as she was.

Tearing her gaze from his, she muttered, "You're an idiot," unsure if she was addressing him or herself. In case it was him, she continued with, "And so is the sheriff for expecting you to go out like this."

"Hikers are missing," he reminded her impatiently.

She rolled her eyes. She'd treated people suffering from

trauma and knew enough about PTSD to be worried about the battle-alert episodes that culminated in dizziness, muscle tremors, sweating and confusion.

"You almost fainted," she pointed out.

"Don't be ridiculous," he snapped, as though she'd suggested something indecent. "SEALs don't faint. I was just a bit dizzy, that's all. I suffer from low blood pressure."

Cassidy looked up at the outrageous lie and shut her mouth on a sigh. Clearly he was in denial. *Fine*. She was just doing her job.

Besides, he was a Navy SEAL. She reminded herself that he did this kind of thing all the time. A shiver slinked up her spine as she pictured him sneaking into hostile territory, wiping everything out before ghosting out again as silently as he'd arrived. She could even picture him—

"What?"

Yeah, Cassidy. What?

Shaking her head, she went back to binding his torso, reminding herself that she didn't need rescuing. She wasn't a damsel in distress and those gold eyes couldn't see into her mind or know what was happening to her.

Except—*darn him*—he probably did. He was no doubt an expert at making women lose their brain cells just by flexing those awesome biceps—or staring at them with that brooding gold gaze. It was no wonder she felt like she was running a fever. It was no wonder her blood was humming through her veins. Her hormone levels were probably shooting through the stratosphere along with her blood pressure.

Finally she fastened the bandage and took a hasty step back, nearly knocking over the table and its contents in her haste to escape. A large hand on her arm kept her upright and when it tightened as she turned away, she looked up. With his gaze on hers, he gently swiped a line of fire across her bottom lip. She gasped and her heart gave a shocked little blip at the unexpected contact.

"Thank you," he said, leaning towards her. And just

when she thought he meant to kiss her, he snagged a plastic container of pain meds behind her. Grinning at the expression on her face, he popped the top, shook a couple into his palm.

He gave a mocking little salute and tossed the container back in the box. "Gotta go," he said, scooping up his clothing in his good hand. With one last heated look in her direction he sauntered from the cell, all long loose-limbed masculine grace, leaving Cassidy staring at the wide expanse of his muscular back and the very interesting way he filled out his faded jeans.

Fortunately, before the outer door could close behind him, Cassidy pulled herself together enough to croak, "You need stitches, Major. I suggest coming to the hospital before you get septicemia and die a horrible death."

Grinning at her over one broad shoulder, he drawled, "It's a date, darlin'," and disappeared, leaving Cassidy with the impression that he had absolutely no intention of following through with his promise.

At least, not for sutures.

CHAPTER THREE

THE SMALL TOWN of Crescent Lake had been established when traders heading north had come over the mountains and found a large crescent-shaped lake nestled in a thickly wooded area. According to Mrs. Krenson at the Lakeside Inn, it had started out as a rough fur-trading town that had gradually grown into the popular tourist town it was today.

The inn, once the local house of pleasure, had been remodeled and modernized over the years. Rising out of a picturesque forest, with mountains at its back and the lake at its feet like a small sparkling sea, it now resembled a gracious, well-preserved old lady, appearing both elegant and mysterious. At least, that's what it said in the brochure and what Cassidy had thought when she'd arrived a few weeks before.

Now, with dark clouds hanging over the valley, the lake was nothing like the crystal-clear mirror it resembled in the pictures and Cassidy had to wish for "sturdy" rather than mysterious.

The day had dawned gray and wet and, standing at her bedroom window, Cassidy couldn't help shivering as she looked up at the mountains shrouded in swirling fog, eerily beautiful and threatening. She wondered if the hikers had been found.

And if she was thinking of a certain someone, it was only because he had no business being out there in the first place. He might be an all-weather hero, but he'd been exhausted, injured and on an edge only he could see. All it would take was one wrong move, one misstep and… And then nothing, she told herself irritably as she spun away from the window. Samuel Kellan was a big boy, a highly trained Navy SEAL. If he wanted to scour the mountains for the next week, it was what he'd been trained for. Heck, he could probably live off the land and heal himself using plants and tree bark.

Whatever effect he'd had on her, Cassidy mused as she closed her bedroom door and headed for the bathroom at the end of the hall, it was over. She'd had the entire night to think about her reaction to him and in the early hours had come to the conclusion that she'd been suffering from low blood sugar…and maybe been a little freaked at finding herself in a jail cell. Maybe even a little awed at meeting a national hero. All perfectly logical explanations for her behavior.

Fortunately she'd recovered, and if she saw him again she'd be the cool, level-headed professional she had a reputation for being. Besides, Samuel J. Kellan was just a man. Like any other.

After a quick shower, she brushed her teeth and headed back to her room to dress. It was her day off and she intended playing tourist. She might have come to the Cascades to escape the mess she'd made of things in Boston, but that didn't mean she had to bury herself in work. Crescent Lake was a beautiful town filled with friendly, curious people who'd brought her baked goodies just to welcome her to town.

She'd read that the Lakefront Boardwalk housed a host of stores that included a few antiques shops, an art gallery selling local artwork, a quaint bookshop and, among others, a cozy coffee shop with a spectacular view of the lake and mountains.

She hadn't had a decent latte since leaving Boston,

and according to the nurses, Just Java served a delicious Caribbean mocha latte, and the triple chocolate muffins were better than sex.

Just what she needed, a double dose of sin.

A soft knock on her door startled her out of her chocolate fantasy and sent her pulse skittering.

"Dr. Mahoney?" a muffled voice called from the hallway. "Cassidy, dear? Are you awake?"

Shrugging into her wrap, Cassidy fastened the tie and shoved damp hair off her forehead. She pulled open the door as a ball of dread settled in her belly. Her landlady wouldn't disturb her unless there was an emergency.

Val Krenson's brows were pinched together over her faded blue eyes and one hand was poised to knock again. "I'm sorry to wake you, dear," she apologized quickly. "That was the hospital. They found the hikers. How soon can you get there?"

"Ten minutes," Cassidy said, already morphing into emergency mode. "Fifteen at the most." She stepped back into the room and would have shut the door but Val held out a hand to detain her.

"John Randal is downstairs, dear. Shall I ask him to wait?"

"That's okay, Val," Cassidy said with a quick shake of her head. "I'll need my car later and I don't want to inconvenience anyone." The last time the deputy had driven her anywhere she'd landed up at the jail. So not going there.

"Planning a little down time?" Val asked with a warm smile.

"It'll have to wait." Cassidy sighed. "They didn't say how serious, did they?"

"I'm afraid not, dear. Just that you get there as soon as possible." She leaned forward. "I'm glad you're here to help Monty out, dear. He tires easily these days." She shook her head. "That man should have retired years ago but not many people want to bury themselves in the mountains."

In some ways Cassidy could understand why. They were a couple of hours from the nearest large town and there wasn't much in the way of nightlife that didn't include a few bars, steakhouses and the local bar and grill, Fahrenheit's.

She might feel like a fish out of water, but she'd been surprised to discover she liked the close-knit community where people knew each other and exchanged gossip with their favorite recipes.

At least here people stopped to chat when they saw you, she thought with a smile, instead of staring right through you as though you didn't exist, or scuttling away like you were an escaped crazy. Surprisingly she was enjoying the slower pace. It was a nice change to be able to connect with the people she was treating. But long term? She didn't know.

"It's a beautiful town, Val, but I've only got a short-term contract."

Val laughed and patted Cassidy's arm. "Don't worry, dear," she said over her shoulder, a twinkle lighting her blue eyes. "I have a feeling you're going to be around a long time."

Cassidy uttered a noncommittal "Hmm" and shut the door behind her landlady. She hunted in the closet for a clean pair of jeans, underwear, socks and a soft green long-sleeved T-shirt. Dressing quickly, she shoved her feet into the nearest pair of boots and grabbed a brush that she hurriedly pulled through her wet hair before piling it on top of her head in a loose style that would dry quickly. Foregoing makeup, she grabbed her medical bag and jacket and headed for the door.

Fifteen minutes after closing the door behind the innkeeper, Cassidy pulled up beside the hospital's staff entrance. Locking her car—which everyone said was unnecessary—she hurried into the waiting room, which was already bustling with chaos and reminded her of a busy city ER.

Her eyes widened. There were people everywhere—sprawled in chairs with their heads tilted back in exhaustion, while even more hovered near the entrance, propping up the walls, slugging back steaming coffee and wolfing down fat sandwiches handed out by a group of women.

Sandwiches? Coffee? And where had all these people come from? It looked like a temporary ops center—or a tea party for big hulking men.

"Good, you're here." A voice at her elbow distracted her from the chaos and Cassidy turned to see the head nurse holding out a clipboard.

She accepted the board, feeling a little shell-shocked. "What on earth's going on?"

Fran Gilbert followed her gaze. "The town's disaster committee in action," she explained with a shrug, as though it happened every day.

Disaster—? Oh, no. Cassidy gulped down a sudden sick feeling. *Please don't tell me...!* Shaking off her pessimistic thoughts, she frowned at the older woman. "Disaster? How bad?"

Fran frowned in confusion. "Bad?" Then realizing what Cassidy was thinking, she said, "*No!* God, no. Cassidy, I'm sorry. I didn't mean to scare you." She gave Cassidy a quick hug. "I just meant that the disaster committee responds whenever the rescue teams go out. The junior league ladies take turns providing hot food and drinks. To practice they set up basic first-aid stations for minor injuries. When news came through that the hikers were being brought down, they moved operations here."

"Oh." Cassidy let out a whoosh of relief, a little awed at the way the community mobilized when the need arose. Any disaster in a big city was met with looting and rioting.

"They say it's to practice for a real disaster but I think it's just an excuse to get out and socialize."

Cassidy nodded. "Okay, no disaster. What *do* we have?" she asked, as Fran led her towards the ER cubicles.

"Mostly minor but too many for poor Monty to cope with," the older woman said, before launching into a rapid-fire report worthy of a busy city ER nurse.

Rebecca Thornton, she told Cassidy, had slipped and fallen off the trail. She'd broken her leg and her husband had climbed down the steep embankment to get to her. He'd slipped near the bottom in the treacherous conditions and knocked himself out. Several others had then climbed down to carry the injured couple out but had found their way blocked by huge boulders. With the gully rapidly filling with water, the group still on the trail had elected to return and alert the authorities. They hadn't made it back yet and a team was still out, looking for them.

Dr. Montgomery looked up briefly from checking a young man's bruised and lacerated arm. "Glad they found you," he said with an absent smile, before turning to give the attending nurse instructions.

Soon Cassidy was swamped, treating a broken leg and collarbone, a fractured wrist and a concussion. There was a bruised and swollen knee that she suspected might be cartilage damage, a host of cuts and scrapes, and hypothermia along with exhaustion and dehydration.

And that was just the hiking party.

Once they'd been examined, treated and transferred to the wards for fluids and observation, Cassidy turned her attention to the rescue crew. Among the expected lacerations and contusions, she diagnosed torn ankle ligaments, a dislocated shoulder and a broken finger. Pretty mild considering the awful night they'd endured, she mused, sending one nurse to the suture room and another to X-rays.

She'd just left Hank Henderson propped up with an ice pack on his foot when the elderly doctor called to ask her opinion about the shoulder injury.

After examining Andy Littleton, Cassidy decided there didn't seem to be any serious ligament damage that would require surgery. She told Andy to take a deep breath and quickly pulled his shoulder back into place. He went white and swayed alarmingly before throwing up in the kidney dish she shoved at him.

Listing drunkenly while she strapped his shoulder and arm, he made Cassidy swear a blood oath that she wouldn't tell anyone he'd cried like a girl. Biting back a grin of sympathy, she squeezed his hand, and turned to find Harry Montgomery beaming at her like a proud teacher whose pupil had surpassed his expectations.

"Looks like old Howie's loss is our gain, eh?" The big man chuckled, his age-spotted hand patting her shoulder awkwardly. "He said you were a bright young thing. What he didn't say was that you have an easy way with people along with that sharp diagnostic mind." He studied her shrewdly. "I guess the old buzzard didn't want to lose you, eh?"

With heat rising to her cheeks, Cassidy looped her stethoscope around her neck. She felt like a new resident under scrutiny. Besides, one didn't have to be Einstein to pick up the question behind the compliment. The question of why she was treating runny noses and middle-ear infections in a small mountain hospital instead of running her own ER—which was what she'd originally intended.

"He's a wonderful man," she replied with a warm smile. "And I loved the daily challenges in ER." Thrusting her hands into her lab-coat pockets, she chose her words carefully. "But big city ERs are like operating in a war zone, and when you lose count of the number of ODs, stabbings and rapes you treat…" She sighed. "I realized I needed a change—to get back to basics. Howie mentioned Crescent Lake and I thought it might be the perfect place to try out something more community-oriented."

She didn't say that hearing it was deep in the Cascades and a continent away from Boston had sounded appealing. She'd been desperate to get away and work on forgetting the career-damaging fallout of treating a real-life hero injured in the line of duty. A "hero" who'd turned out to be anything but.

She shuddered at the memory. *God*, she'd been stupidly naïve and had paid a very high price. Then again, how could anyone have known the handsome vice cop wasn't one of the good guys?

The charming wounded-hero act had been just that—an act. He'd used it to lull people—*her*—into a false sense of security. He'd pursued her with flowers, gifts and romantic dinners then stolen her hospital security card, giving him access to the ER dispensary as well as a stack of prescription pads, which he'd used by forging her signature. In the end there'd been a full-scale police investigation—with her as the prime suspect.

In truth, all she'd really been guilty of had been bad judgment. She'd trusted someone who'd proved to be anything *but* trustworthy. In hindsight he'd been too good to be true: too romantic and too sensitive for it not to have been a very clever performance from a man who knew exactly what women wanted.

By the time she'd realized something was wrong, the media frenzy had crucified her, calling her professional competence into question. It had been a nightmare.

Fortunately for her, Lance Turnbull had been under internal investigation. One that had involved a dozen other women doctors around the city. Cassidy had eventually been cleared of all charges but the damage had been done. She'd suffered through snide comments and cruel jokes from her colleagues until she'd finally buckled under the stress.

"GP work is pretty boring compared to the excitement of ER," the old doctor warned, wrenching her from her disturbing thoughts. "Especially here in the boondocks."

Relieved to focus on something other than her past failures, Cassidy looked around at the controlled chaos and sent him a small smile. "I wouldn't exactly call it boring," she said, her smile turning into a grin when his deep chuckle filled the hallway.

"No, it isn't," he agreed, "especially during tourist season. But off season gets pretty quiet."

"I can do quiet. And I'm impressed with the way everyone bands together. It's wonderful knowing that there are still places where people are willing to step in and help their neighbors without expecting something in return."

"That's what's kept me here for sixty years," he said, moving to the door. "The warm community spirit. You don't find that in the city." He turned and studied her intently. "I've watched you over the past two weeks, Cassidy, and you're a very perceptive diagnostician. We could use someone like you heading up the hospital." And when Cassidy opened her mouth to remind him that she was only there for three months, he beat her to it with his parting shot, "Think about it," before disappearing down the hallway.

Cassidy watched him leave. Admittedly she was enjoying the opportunity to practice family medicine in a town where people cared about each other, but Boston was her home. And that kind of decision couldn't be made lightly.

It wasn't until late afternoon that she finally realized she'd been hanging around waiting for something to happen. It didn't take a genius to realize that *something* was a certain Navy SEAL and that she'd been waiting for him to come in to have his injuries treated.

Irritated with herself, she'd collected her purse and jacket and was on her way out when the door banged open and there he was, looking like he'd just blown in from a big, bad superheroes convention with his big, bad SEAL attitude.

When her knees wobbled and her head went light, Cassidy assured herself it was simply because she hadn't eaten anything all day. It certainly didn't have anything to do

with the way his gold eyes latched onto her like a trac-
tor beam.

Gesturing to an empty suture room, Cassidy wordlessly
handed her jacket and purse to the receptionist and ignored the jitters in her belly as the sheriff half-dragged,
half-carried him down the corridor and through the doorway to heave him onto the narrow bed. And just like that,
every delusional thought she'd had in the early hours blew
up right in her face.

"You may now stick him with as many needles as you
like," the sheriff announced, shoving his hands on his hips
and glaring at his brother. "In fact, that's an official order.
Maybe it will improve his attitude and I won't have to toss
him in jail again for disobeying a direct order."

"I said I was fine," the SEAL snarled as Greg, the young
deputy who'd helped drag him into the examination room,
ducked his head and made a beeline for the door.

Wise move, she thought when a string of muttered
threats turned the air blue. She might be relieved he'd made
it back in one piece but it had been a long day and an even
longer night, obsessing about whether or not she had been
imagining things. The good news was that she was sane
and not hallucinating. The bad news was, Cassidy thought
with a sinking sensation, he was even more dangerously
attractive in the cold light of day.

And that was bad. Very bad. Because Cassidy Mahoney
was done with dangerous bad boys who made women
swoon. She really was too busy getting her life back to
deal with two hundred and forty pounds of belligerent male.

It seemed the sheriff was too since he folded his arms
across his chest and glared at his brother, clearly not intimidated by the show of aggression. "And if he gives you
any trouble, make him wear a pretty pink hospital gown,"
he barked, ignoring the way Sam's lip drew back over his
teeth in a silent snarl. "He deserves to have everyone laugh
at his ugly butt after the stunt he pulled."

Cassidy watched the silent clash of wills and her first thought was that nothing about Major Kellan was ugly. She was pretty sure her staff wouldn't be laughing either. More like swooning from the thick cloud of testosterone and bad attitude that surrounded him.

A fierce golden gaze caught and held hers as though he knew what she was thinking, and Cassidy felt a flush creep up her neck into her cheeks. Besides being grossly unprofessional, picturing him naked wouldn't do a thing to convince her she'd imagined her earlier reaction to him.

The sheriff raked his hand through his wet hair, looking tired and exasperated. "Listen up, man," he growled, "I know you're a big, mean SEAL and everything, but just let the doc check you out, okay? I don't have time to babysit you or keep you from bleeding to death. You wouldn't believe the paperwork. It's a nightmare. Elections are coming up and I can't afford to have you die and make me look bad."

"I keep telling you I'm fine," Sam snarled. "Quit hovering like a girl. There's nothing Old Monty can do that I can't do for myself, so get the hell out of my face before I break your ugly mug."

"Oh, please." Ruben snickered rudely. "You can't even break a sweat without help. Now suck it up and let the doc check you out. You look like hell."

Samuel said something that Cassidy was pretty sure was anatomically impossible but before her eyes could do more than widen, Ruben turned to her with a grim smile. "Doc, he's all yours, just as I promised. He's a bit more battered and bloodied but I refuse to take credit for that. He's a hard-headed pain in the ass so you might consider sedating him." He sent his brother a meaningful glare. "In fact, unconscious would be a real improvement."

Ignoring the derisive suggestion, Sam turned narrowed eyes her way. "Doc?" he demanded. "You're the *doctor*?" His tone suggested she'd deliberately misled him. "I thought you were the nurse."

"No," she corrected smoothly. "You thought I was a stripper."

"And with that," Ruben drawled mockingly, "I rest my case." He slapped his hat on his head and adjusted the brim. "Cassidy, ignore the inscrutable death stares. Underneath all that macho SEAL *hoo-yah* attitude he's really quite sweet."

The SEAL snarled something impolite and with a deep laugh the sheriff sketched a salute and disappeared down the hallway, leaving Cassidy with two hundred pounds of seething testosterone. Sweet wasn't a word she'd associate with Major Hotstuff, she mused, moving to the supply cabinet for a towel. Just the idea of it made her want to smile. So she frowned instead.

"So," he said, taking the towel and fixing her with his mesmerizing stare, "you're a doctor."

She sent him a cool look then turned to remove disinfectant and a package of swabs from the overhead cabinet. "Is that a problem, Major, or an apology?"

His amused gaze drifted over her face and breasts to the neat row of supplies she'd begun setting out and he drawled, "Only if you're plotting revenge."

"Fortunately for you I'm not the vengeful type, Major."

His mouth curled at one corner and he said, "Uh-huh" into the towel. Cassidy ignored the impulse to bang her head against the wall. She had a feeling it would be a lot less painful than getting caught up in the man's web.

Fortunately, her little chat with the elderly doctor had reminded her of why she was off men in anything but the professional sense. Flicking him an assessing glance, she decided the sheriff was right. He did look like hell.

"There's no one to save you from the needle this time, Major." She opened another cabinet and removed a suture kit and syringes. "In fact—" her voice was brisk as she moved closer "—I can foresee more than one in your immediate future."

Ignoring the dark eyebrow hiking up his forehead, she stepped close and pushed the soaked parka over his wide shoulders and down his arms. He shrugged and sucked in a sharp breath, before drawling, "Not just beautiful and smart, but psychic too?"

Cassidy bit back a snort and tossed the garment onto the floor, before turning to wash her hands at the small basin. "It doesn't take a clairvoyant to see that you're an action junkie looking for trouble," she replied smoothly, pulling a strip off the paper towel dispenser.

He shrugged. "Goes with the job."

"For which the free world is eternally grateful." She dried her hands and dropped the paper into the bin as she turned. She caught his eyes crinkling at the corners as though he didn't take himself half as seriously as other people did, which…surprised her. She was accustomed to being surrounded by alpha males who thought they sat at God's right hand. Discovering he could poke fun at himself had something warm and light sliding into her belly. Something that felt very much like admiration.

Telling herself that certainly didn't mean she *liked* him, Cassidy focused on his once white T-shirt, now covered in mud and blood. Shaking her head, she pulled it out of his damp waistband and grabbed a pair of scissors off the counter.

With a few snips, his shirt fell away and she quickly unwound the soiled bandage. When the move exposed fresh blood oozing from the loosened dressing, she bit back a curse.

"You're an idiot," she muttered, knowing exactly who she was addressing this time. Lifting a loose edge, she pressed her hand gently against his hard belly and ripped it off in one smooth move.

Sam hissed audibly in surprise and pain. "*Holy…!* Hell

and damnation, woman, what the *hell* was that?" His fingers whitened around the edge of the bed and he looked like he wanted to wrap them around her throat.

"Sorry," she said, and meaning it. It would have been worse if she'd taken her time removing it. "It's better coming off fast."

"For you maybe… *Jeez*…does the CIA know about you?"

"The CIA?" she asked, sending him a narrow-eyed look out the corner of her eye, fairly certain he wasn't being complimentary.

"Yeah. Hear they're looking for interrogators." Definitely not complimentary. "My CO would recruit you on the spot to torture the tadpoles in BUD/S."

"Tadpoles? Buds?" she asked, pouring disinfectant into a stainless-steel bowl and filling it with warm water.

"Wannabe SEALs in Basic Underwater Demolition SEALs," he told her. "Have to knock the cra…I mean stuffing out of them during hell week to sort out the men from the boys. You'd be perfect for the job."

Apparently *he'd* managed to survive without having the stuffing knocked out of him. She wondered how he'd managed it. Sheer stubbornness most likely.

She pulled on a pair of latex gloves then ripped off a large section of cotton wool. "I'm good, but thanks anyway." She pressed a hand to the smooth ball of his shoulder. "Lie flat and lift your arm over your head."

His scowl turned into a grimace when he realized he was too big and had to scoot down the bed, ending up with half his long legs draped over the end. Growling irritably about "damn midget beds", he raised his arm and bent it behind his head. With lids lowered over his unusual eyes, he sent her a sleepy look.

"Although if you continue ripping off my clothes and making me lie down," he drawled softly, "I'll start thinking you have ulterior motives, Miz Honey."

"That's *Dr.* Mahoney to you," she said absently, carefully cleaning the area around the wound before selecting another wad of gauze to clean the wound itself. It would take about a dozen stitches to close.

"Yes, *ma'am.*" His voice was polite and subdued but a quick look caught the irreverent smirk curling his mouth. Cassidy swallowed the impulse to return that impudent grin. Or worse—kiss his battered mouth better. From all accounts he was the kind of man who wouldn't stop at kissing. From all accounts he was only interested in quick tumbles with the nearest available woman. Probably because being a SEAL precluded any kind of stable or long-term relationship.

She shivered. If she knew what was good for her, she'd shove her libido back into hibernation and stop getting all excited every time he invaded her space.

Dr. Mahoney was back in charge, she reminded herself, and there would be no mixing her chemistry with his. On *any* level. She was going to patch him up, send him on his way, and hope like hell she never saw him again.

CHAPTER FOUR

SAM WATCHED DOC BOSTON work on his torso and wondered why he was so drawn to a woman who made it abundantly clear she wasn't interested. He tried reminding himself that he'd be heading back to Coronado soon and anything more than harmless flirting was impossible. It didn't help. Not even when he observed the competent way she wielded sharp objects.

Sure, she was beautiful but then, so were a million other women, and he'd had little problem leaving them behind. Except there was something compelling about her that told Sam she wouldn't be easy to forget or walk away from. She was smart and mouthy and didn't take his reputation as a badass seriously or treat him differently from other patients. And *that* more than anything made him like her.

Okay, he *really* liked the look of her—he was a guy, so sue him—but lately all the feminine adulation had begun to irritate him. All a lot of women saw was a SEAL with hard muscles and weird eyes. A guy they could brag about being with to their friends. He'd enjoyed that in his twenties, but in the decade since he'd seen and done things no one should see or do.

Cassidy Mahoney, on the other hand, did more of the squinty-eye thing that for some strange reason made him want to smile when he hadn't felt the urge in a long, long time. It made him want to push her up against the nearest wall and taste all that soft, smooth skin.

He thought of how she'd react if he acted on the impulse, and had to suppress a grin when her suspicion-filled look said she knew what he was thinking. His what-have-I-done-now eyebrow-lift had her eyes narrowing, as if she suspected he was up to no good. A flush rose from the lapels of her lab coat and climbed her neck into her cheeks.

If she only knew.

"I promise not to wrestle you to the ground and stab you in the throat with that," he assured her, then decided to qualify it with, "Well...maybe wrestle you to the ground..." His gaze smoothed over her breasts and up her long throat to her lush mouth. "Okay, *definitely* wrestle you to the ground. But the stabbing thing? You're safe. SEAL's honor."

She didn't disappoint him. Thrusting out a plump lower lip that he yearned to take a greedy bite out of, she huffed out an annoyed breath that disturbed the long tendrils of fine silvery hair escaping her tousled topknot. She appeared at once exasperated, embarrassed and incredibly appealing.

"Give it a rest, Major." She huffed again, shoving the needle into a vial of local anesthetic like she was probably imagining it was his hide. He covered a wince by scratching his chin. "It must be exhausting trying to keep that up."

"Keep what up?" he asked innocently, wanting her to keep talking. Even rife with irritation, he liked the sound of her voice—smooth and silky, like hundred-year-old bourbon. It intoxicated his senses and kept him from thinking about gut-wrenching guilt and things he couldn't change.

She removed the needle and flicked the syringe a couple of times before gently depressing the plunger. A tiny spurt fountained from the tip. "The seduction routine," she said, wiping an area close to his wound with an alcohol swab. "Heaven knows, just trying to keep up with it is exhausting."

"It's really no trouble," he assured her, except lately

it *had* become exhausting. Most likely he was just out of practice. Life-and-death situations didn't leave much time for fun and games. "I can do it in my sleep."

She gently slid the needle into his flesh. There was a tiny pinch and almost instantly cold numbness began to spread along his side. He sighed with relief as she removed the needle and pressed a small swab over the puncture wound.

"That's the problem, isn't it?" she murmured, tossing the syringe into the nearby medical waste container. She opened the suture kit onto a strip of newly torn paper toweling. "It's meaningless."

He shrugged and this time couldn't prevent a wince from escaping. Last night he'd wrenched his shoulder hauling an injured man up a slippery cliff face. "Women seem to like it," he said on a yawn, deciding he really liked the way her wide green eyes went all squinty and irritated when he piled on the charm. It made him want to lay it on extra-thick just to see her scowl at him.

She made a noise that sounded like a snort and he had to clench his jaw to keep from grinning with satisfaction. "They probably don't want to hurt your feelings," she pointed out.

"You think so?" He tried the wounded look but he suspected she wasn't fooled.

"This is not the eighties," she informed him with a *get-real* lift of an eyebrow. "Not all women appreciate being charmed out of their panties with lines from a bad movie script."

He looked skeptical and she shook her head as though he was beyond help. Sam waited until she turned back with a suture needle and monofilament thread, before handing her needle scissors. He watched surprise flit across her face and knew what she was thinking. *What did a macho idiot know about needle scissors?* He grimaced. *Other than having first-hand experience?*

"I went to med school," he reminded her, when she made

no move to take them. He was annoyed for caring about her opinion—which had been pretty obvious from the outset, thanks to the sheriff locking him in a jail cell for no good reason.

"The way I hear it," she said, accepting the instrument as well as the implied reproach with a nod, "you cut med school to play pirates." He watched her get a firm grip on the needle and press the edges of his skin together with her left hand. She pushed the needle through, released it and gripped it with the flat edge of the scissors, before carefully pulling it free.

"You shouldn't believe everything you hear," he advised darkly, talking about more than embellished stories of his SEAL exploits. He had a feeling someone had been filling her head with his youthful indiscretions—*most* of which were gross exaggerations, the rest outright lies.

Her open skepticism confirmed his suspicions. "You mean you don't wear a cape and fly around the world in your underwear, saving humanity?" Her movements were quick and confident and a neat row of stitches began closing the three-inch slash on his belly.

Sam chuckled and thanked God for BDUs. It was kind of nice having a conversation with a woman who didn't treat him like he walked on water or was there to scratch her itch. It was even better watching her full pink mouth when she talked. It made him think of long dark nights, crisp cool sheets and hot wet kisses when he hadn't thought about them in a while. It was a relief to discover he was still normal in one important area.

"You don't believe that, do you?"

She deftly tied off and started on a fourth suture. "I stopped believing in superheroes a long time ago, Major," she said absently. She looked up and caught his gaze. "So why *did* you?"

"Why did I what?"

"Join the Navy instead of finishing med school."

"I did finish," he told her, "courtesy of Uncle Sam."

"But why the armed forces when you were already doing something that would save lives?"

He fought a knee-jerk reaction to come up with some stupid macho excuse that would confirm her not so flattering opinion of him. But something held him back. Something deep inside wanted very much for her to think of him as more than a battered sailor with big muscles.

"I was in New York when the Towers fell," he said, wincing as the words emerged. He'd never shared his true reasons with anyone but for some reason found himself spilling his guts to her.

He remembered exactly what he'd been doing when his safe world had fallen apart. He'd been living the life of a typical student, concerned only with enjoying the hell out of being young, healthy and surrounded by girls and parties.

"You…you were *there*?"

Sam looked up, almost surprised to find he wasn't alone. Cassidy's green eyes were huge and filled with a compassion he knew he didn't deserve.

"A few blocks away," he said impassively. "I'd cut class and was staying in Brooklyn with a friend for a few days. We were sitting at a sidewalk café, having coffee and bagels, when…when the first plane flew into the towers." He fell silent for a couple beats before continuing. "We tried getting through but the cops stopped us. Never felt so helpless in my life. There I was, a fourth-year med student thinking I had it all."

His lips twisted self-deprecatingly. "Thinking I *knew* it all." He speared her with a haunted look. "I saw many draw their last breaths. I don't ever want to feel that helpless again. The next day Jack and I enlisted. We were determined to take a more active role in protecting our country."

"Healing the sick and saving people *is* taking an active

role, Major," she reminded him, but he was already shaking his head.

"Not active enough, Doc. Besides, there are thousands of civilian doctors Stateside," he pointed out. "What about the men and women protecting our country? Protecting the free world? Who saves them?"

"I…"

"My friend's father was one of the firefighters killed that day," he continued, as though she hadn't interrupted. "I'll never forget the look on Jack's face when he heard his dad was never coming home." Sam closed his eyes on remembered devastation—of that day as well as events more recent than 9/11. "You never forget that kind of pain."

You never forget, Sam admitted silently. *And the guilt eats at you that you are alive and they aren't.*

Cassidy watched as fierce emotions moved across his features, through his beautiful eyes. She felt a little pinch in the region of her heart. Crescent Lake's hero was hurting, and the discovery that he was more than just a pretty face and a hot body terrified her in ways that she didn't want to analyze.

She'd rather think of him as a shallow womanizer who'd enlisted because men in uniform got more girls. Although, in or out of uniform, the man would attract more than his share of women.

Using her wrist to push away the tendrils of hair that kept obscuring her vision, Cassidy studied him closely. The events of 9/11 may have changed the course of his life, but she had a feeling something more recent had put that *haunted* look in his eyes. And suddenly, more than anything, she wanted them glinting wickedly at her again.

Whoa, she warned herself silently when the notion seemed more appealing than it should. *Way too intense for someone you can't wait to get away from.*

In silence, she completed another suture before asking casually, "So you didn't?"

His muscles bunched beneath her fingers and he went strangely still for a couple of beats before asking, "Didn't what?"

There was a sudden shift in the air and she felt the hair at her nape rise. Primitive warning whooshed up her spine and she sucked in a sharp breath. Lifting her head, she found his attention locked on her—laser bright and strangely intent. It was odd, feeling as though they were communicating on different levels, only one of which was verbal. And even more disturbing to realize that she didn't have a clue what it was all about.

"Cut med school to play pirates on the high seas," she reminded him, and watched, mesmerized, as his big body relaxed. His gaze lost that fierce glitter and his mouth its tight, forbidding line, even going so far as to kick up at one corner. The air surrounding them shifted again and she was left dizzied by the sudden shifts in mood.

His teeth flashed white in his dark face. "Well…technically…I suppose I did."

Cassidy sighed and concentrated on the last suture. "You're an idiot." Sam snorted, apparently as relieved as she was to lighten the tension. The band of pressure around her skull eased a little more. She really, *really*, didn't want to like him. At least, not any more than she already did. That would be so utterly irresponsible—not to mention stupid.

"That's the third time you've said that," he accused plaintively.

"I meant it before too."

His eyes crinkled at the corners. "Why? Because I like to jump out of airplanes?"

"No," she said, unlacing his mud-caked boot and dropping it on the floor, along with his wet sock. "Because you blow people up instead of healing them." She retrieved a stool from the corner and slid it under his hard calf, reaching for a pair of scissors. There was no way she was going to wrestle him out of his wet jeans to get to the thigh injury. Just the thought of him lying there in his underwear—*God, did he even wear them?*—gave her a hot flash.

"I do heal people," he said mildly as she began cutting the wet denim. "All spec ops teams need medics."

She paused and frowned at him. "Well, why aren't you doing *this*…" she gestured to the room around them "… instead of wreaking havoc and blowing things up?"

His expression clearly questioned her intelligence. "I just told you. Besides, I like blowing things up," he said as though she was a particularly dense blonde, and she wanted to smack him. She had a sneaky suspicion that had been his intention. It seemed he was as eager as she was to move away from intensely personal subjects. "And I'm good at wreaking havoc."

Cassidy rolled her eyes and said, "You are such a guy," with such feminine disgust that Sam laughed.

"And that's bad, how?"

He was so delusional that she stared silently at him for a couple of beats as though she couldn't believe what she was hearing.

Besides, the man's blood was probably ninety-nine percent testosterone and she'd been lucky to escape unscathed the first time around. Well, not completely unscathed, she admitted reluctantly, but she had a feeling if she allowed Samuel Kellan to matter, she wouldn't be so lucky. "It's bad when you won't talk about what's bothering you."

He snorted and sent her a look that said she was delusional. "Talking's for politicians…and girls," he scoffed, and she huffed out an exasperated breath, suspecting that he was being insulting on purpose. *Sneaky.* "SEALs are doers," he continued. "They don't do a lot of standing around, talking. If they did, nothing would get done." His eyes crinkled and his grin turned wicked. "But if you want to know what I was thinking last night, I'd be happy—"

"I *know* what you were thinking," Cassidy quickly interrupted, slicing through tough, wet denim towards his knee. "Clearly your seduction techniques need adjusting."

He grinned and said, "Oh, yeah?" before waggling his eyebrows in a comical way that had her rolling her eyes. When she stopped checking out the state of her brain she found him studying her with an intensity that had her pulse hitching then picking up its pace. The man's mercurial mood changes made her dizzy.

"I'm talking about whatever it is that has you brooding when you think no one's looking," she said casually, as though she was just making conversation to take his mind off what she was about to do. "I'm talking about reacting to sharp stimuli like you're expecting a ninja attack." Something dark and haunted flickered in his gaze before his expression hardened. "Plenty of people suffer from PTSD, Major," she continued casually, as she hacked through the denim to his knee. "It's nothing to be ashamed of."

He made a rude sound. "You're a shrink now?" he drawled, and Cassidy continued as though he hadn't spoken. "I specialized in trauma medicine. People who survive traumatic experiences come through ER on a daily basis. It's very common."

"Just being a SEAL exposes you to stressful situations," Sam interrupted impatiently. "It's the job. If you can't deal, you have no business being a SEAL. So you deal. End of story." He was silent a moment and she felt the air shift again. "Besides, I like blowing things up, remember."

He clearly didn't intend to say anything more, but that was okay, Cassidy reflected. At least next time—*if* there was a next time—she could bring it up when he was in a better frame of mind. For now she'd respect his need to avoid the subject.

Lifting the denim at his knee to make the final cuts, she acknowledged quietly, "Yes, I remember."

She'd barely exposed his mid-thigh when he flinched and grabbed her hand with an alarmed "*Whoa.*" He'd clamped his free hand over his crotch and was eyeing the scissors like she was holding a live grenade.

Cassidy rolled her eyes and gently peeled away the blood-soaked denim, grimacing at the jagged gash on his hard thigh. "This is going to hurt," she said, reaching for disinfectant and cotton wool. After liberally dousing the area, she probed the wound gently, before injecting a pain-killer into his thigh.

"So," he murmured when she'd tied off the first suture and was starting on the second, "what's a big-city ER girl doing in a place like this?"

Cassidy flashed him an exasperated look and deftly maneuvered the needle scissors as she completed another suture. "We've already had this conversation, remember?"

Sam scratched his chin and the rasp of his stubble sent a shiver of awareness down her spine. It reminded her of how virile and dangerous he was to her peace of mind. "I was a little tired last night."

"Uh-huh," Cassidy said dryly, and tied off the next suture.

"You never did answer the question, though," Sam pressed, before she could ask about his sleeping habits. He looked more exhausted and drawn than a single night without sleep warranted. And with his other symptoms, he was most likely having nightmares as well.

She studied him intently. "What question?"

"You. Here in the boondocks."

Cassidy turned away from his keen gaze and sorted through a box of dressings. She needed a few moments to gather her composure. After selecting what she needed, she turned with a shrug. "Big-city burn-out. I just needed a change."

"Ahhh," Sam drawled, as she tore open the packaging with more force than was necessary.

"What's that supposed to mean?" she demanded, stripping off the backing and gently pressing it over the sutures on his belly.

He grimaced. "Romance gone bad."

Cassidy gave a shocked laugh, staggered by his perception, and dropped her gaze to his thigh. She knew what he was doing. And, boy, was his diversion effective. "Believe me, romance is *way* off base."

"Then…?"

Rattled, Cassidy sucked in a steadying breath then answered, "Let's just say I needed to find some perspective."

"Yeah," he said softly, his eyes taking on a bleak expression that had her own problems vanishing in the sudden urge to wrap her arms around him. His mouth twisted in a sad, bitter smile. "God knows, I'm acquainted with perspective."

Unsure how to respond in a way that wouldn't have her coming across as an emotional wreck, Cassidy silently went back to work. Besides, what was there to say? Fortunately, he didn't seem to have any clue either. By the time she'd finished he seemed to have slipped into sleep but when she eased away, he groaned and sat up.

A quick glance over her shoulder caught his grimace of pain. His jaw bunched and he grabbed the side tattooed with bruises as he swung his legs over the side. Having finally come off his adrenaline high, he was pale, exhausted and hurting.

"I'll get you some pain meds," she said quietly, turning away to reach into the overhead cabinet. She heard a faint sound and felt the air shift at her back an instant before heat spread along her shoulders and down to the backs of her thighs. Her pulse leapt, her chest went tight and it was all she could do to keep from turning into his big, hard body. To lean on him and let him lean on her.

A long tanned arm reached over her shoulder and he snagged a bottle of pain meds. "This'll do," he said, his voice gravel-rough and sexy. She felt his gaze and turned her head, slowly lifting her gaze up his tanned throat to the hard line of his shadowed jaw, past his poet's mouth and strong straight nose.

He was close. Too close. His gold eyes darkened and something vibrated and snapped between them. Something deep and primal. Something so incendiary she was surprised her clothes didn't catch fire.

Cassidy opened her mouth to say—*God, she didn't have a clue*—then snapped it shut when nothing emerged. The air around them abruptly heated and to her horror his eyes went all hot and sleepy. He felt it too, she realized, and all she had to do was shift a couple of inches closer…and their mouths would—

No sooner had the thought formed than Sam was moving, and before she could do more than squeak out a protest, he'd spun her around and pushed her up against the wall and the heat became a liquid fire in her blood.

She saw his lips moving but heard nothing past the rush of blood filling her ears. Her palms tingled, her body tensed in anticipation and time slowed as his head dipped. Then his mouth was closing over hers and everything…*everything*…sound, heat, sensation…was rushing at her like she'd entered a time warp and was speeding towards something destructive…and wildly exhilarating.

Shock was her first reaction, her second was "*Hmmf…*" When she realized her palms were flat against his hard belly, she tried to shove him away. She didn't want this. It was too much, too little and…*God*…too *everything*. Instinctively she knew that if she let him continue, he'd suck her into his force-field and she'd burn up in the impact. But then he lifted his head and his battered lips brushed across hers, soothingly and so sweetly, and her resistance crumbled.

With a low growl she felt in the pit of her belly, his mouth descended, opening over hers to consume every thought in her head and pull the oxygen from her lungs, leaving her senses spinning.

She heard a low, husky moan and realized with a sense of alarm that it had come from her. *God…*she never moaned. *Ever.* But, then, she'd never been kissed like her soul was being sucked from her body.

She clutched at him to keep from sliding to the floor and an answering groan filled the air, cocooning them in heated silence. This time she was certain it wasn't her.

Tunneling long fingers into her hair, Samuel wrapped them around her skull to tip her head so he could change the angle of the kiss. Instantly his tongue slid past her lips to tangle with hers. Cassidy's breath hitched, her mouth softened and her eyes drifted closed. As if she welcomed the all-encompassing heat.

And, God, how could she not? She'd never felt anything like it. It was like being suspended in a thick, heated silence with nothing but the taste of him in her mouth, the hard feel of him against her, the sound of her pounding pulse filling her head, while heat and wildness rushed through her veins.

And just when her body flowed against his and she thought she would pass out from lack of oxygen, he broke the kiss and murmured a stunned *"What the hell…?"* between dragging desperate breaths into his lungs.

Confused by the sudden retreat, a small frown creased the smooth skin of her forehead and her eyes fluttered open to see his gaze burning into hers with a fierce intensity—as though he blamed her for the tilting of the earth.

For long stunned moments he stared at her like he'd never seen her before. Then, so abruptly her knees buckled, he shoved away from the wall and retreated, leaving her feeling like he'd drawn back his fist and slugged her in the head.

"Wh-what…? Why…?" Great, now she was stuttering. She gulped and tried again. "What the hell was that?"

Angling his body, Sam folded his arms across his chest and propped his shoulder against the wall where not seconds ago he'd had her pinned. Abruptly inscrutable, his arched brow questioned her sanity.

After a long moment his gaze dropped to her mouth again. "I had to see if you taste as delicious as you look," he drawled, as though it was perfectly normal to push someone up against a wall and suck the air from their lungs.

Infuriated with the quiver in her belly and the urge to slide back against the wall with him, Cassidy shoved at the hair that had been disturbed by his marauding fingers and glared back at him. "Look," she snapped, "I'm not some brainless Navy bunny desperate to trade passable kisses with a hot Navy SEAL. I haven't the time or the inclination and this is certainly *not* the place."

His eyes narrowed in challenge and for a second she thought he'd get mad, but finally his mouth slid into a slow, sexy grin. "*Hot?*" His eyebrows waggled. "You think I'm *hot?*"

And she wanted to slug him.

Deciding to escape before she did or said something she would regret, Cassidy headed for the door on shaky legs. She paused with a cool look over her shoulder, as if she hadn't just had her tongue in his mouth. *Not going to think about that.*

"If you feel feverish or the area surrounding your injuries becomes inflamed and swollen," she said curtly in parting, "phone in for a prescription. Otherwise make an appointment to have those stitches removed in a week."

CHAPTER FIVE

SAM STOOD BEHIND the solid oak bar and mixed cocktails for a table of women in the corner near the dance floor. It was their second set of drinks for what looked like some kind of ritual girls' night out. Gifts were piled in the corners of the booth, leading him to surmise it was either someone's birthday or a bachelorette party.

He just hoped they didn't get out of hand and start dancing on the tables and shedding their clothes or he'd be forced to throw them out. Some of the male customers tended to get a little upset when he broke up impromptu floor shows, but even in Crescent Lake the sheriff's department frowned on that kind of behavior. The last time it had happened he'd ended up in a jail cell at the mercy of an evil blonde.

Shifting to ease the pressure on his injured thigh, Sam nodded to a few old acquaintances and poured a cosmopolitan into a martini glass.

He'd never understood how any self-respecting adult could order cocktails called orgasms or pink panthers, let alone drink them. He was a strictly beer and malt kind of guy and the thought of slugging back sickly-sweet concoctions the color of candy floss was enough to make him gag. Of course he'd also been known to toss back the occasional tequila with his buddies—but only as a matter of pride.

An off-duty deputy called out, "Hey, Sam," as he pushed

his way through the crowd, arm slung across the shoulders of a hot babe in tight jeans and even tighter tank top. Sam responded with an eye-waggle in the woman's direction and Hank grinned, calling out, "She's got a friend. Interested?"

Sam laughed and shook his head. His sister wasn't due in till ten, but until then he was in charge. It was only a little after eight and Fahrenheit's was already packed. He could hardly hear himself think over the sound of music pouring from the jukebox. The band was busy setting up but wasn't due to start until nine and the kitchen was pushing out huge platters of buffalo wings, fries and chili hot enough to singe the varnish off the bar.

He'd spent the entire week rescuing stray cattle, hauling in joyriders and dodging buckshot from old man Jeevers, who thought the deputies were aliens beamed down from the mother ship. And when he wasn't playing cop he'd worked the taps behind the bar, listening to Jerry Farnell recount his experiences in Desert Storm.

His brother had talked him into "helping out" at the sheriff's office, but Sam wasn't fooled. Ruben wanted some fraternal bonding time so he could casually talk about why Sam was home, acting like a moody bastard instead of parachuting into hostile territory and sneaking up on bad guys.

He suspected his family had formed a tag team to work on him, hoping he'd crack and spill his guts. They were clearly as tired of his bad attitude as his CO had become. Heck, *he* was tired of his bad attitude. He wanted to get back to the teams, doing what he'd been trained for.

What they didn't understand was that SEALs didn't crack under pressure or talk about their missions. What they did was mostly classified so they *couldn't* talk. Besides, he'd seen and done some pretty bad things that he didn't want to think too hard about. *Ever.* If he did he'd go crazy and end up like Jerry, propping up a bar somewhere, getting drunk while reliving his glory days.

Finally, the bozos taking up one side of the bar got tired of trying to provoke him and turned their attention to speculating about the fancy Boston babe helping out at the hospital.

He eventually stopped listening to their inventive illnesses just to have "five minutes alone with her so I can drop my shorts and show the little lady what a *real* man looks like."

Sam snorted. Doc Boston might have come to town to "get some perspective" but he suspected her *perspective* didn't include checking out the local talent. She was a beautiful, classy woman who'd probably seen countless men drop their shorts, and an idiot like Buddy Holliday would hardly impress her. Besides, her reaction to *his* kiss had told him he'd been right. Some guy had worked her over and she was taking it out on him.

Except in his experience a woman didn't always need a reason to act like a man was a pervert for pushing her up against the wall and sucking the air from her lungs. They often behaved irrationally for no apparent reason—which was why he enjoyed being a SEAL. Guys didn't mind if you scratched yourself in public, and burping was an accepted form of male bonding.

Furthermore, before she'd stormed off, bristling, with insult, she'd had her beautiful body pressed against his, her hands in his hair and her tongue in his mouth—and had enjoyed every hot minute of it, no matter what she'd said.

The good news was people suffering from PTSD didn't dream or fantasize about kissing a woman until her muscles went fluid and her breath hitched in her throat. They didn't obsess about running their hands through long, silky hair or down smooth, sleek thighs and they sure as hell didn't have erotic dreams about someone who treated them like she wanted to slide her lush curvy body up against you one minute then scrape you off the bottom of her shoe the next.

He'd be insane to even consider pursuing someone who

ripped off a dozen layers of skin along with an adhesive dressing. And, contrary to popular opinion, Sam Kellan wasn't insane.

Fortunately someone called his name and Sam turned, grateful for the distraction. He'd spent way too much time thinking about her as it was.

Over the next hour he kept the drinks coming and tried to work up some enthusiasm for the trio of woman bellied up to the bar, heavily made-up eyes currently stripping him naked and acting like he should feel flattered.

He didn't. He'd learned early that women liked Navy SEALs. They liked their big muscles and hard bodies and they liked their stamina. He mostly liked women too, but tonight he wasn't in the mood to oblige them.

By the time his sister arrived for her shift, he was ready to head off into the wilderness to get away from people for a while. "Where the hell have you been?" he demanded, in a tone that had her welcoming smile morph into a confused frown.

"What are you talking about?"

"You're late."

Hannah flicked her attention to the wall clock. "Fifteen minutes. Big deal. And quit scowling like that, you're scaring away my customers." She looked over the happy crowd and noticed the group of men cozied up to the bar, scarfing down buffalo wings, and grimaced when she recognized them. "What did Buddy say to upset you?" she demanded, eyeing him cautiously, like she expected him to morph into a psycho.

"I'm not upset." *Yeesh*, what was with women lately? "Women get upset, guys get mad."

She rolled her eyes. "Fine, what are you *mad* about now?"

"I'm not mad. Listening to them yap about the length of their johns and betting on who's going to score first is giving me a brain bleed."

"So? They do that every week. Last week it was with that group of coeds from Olympia. You thought it was pretty damn funny then and told me to chill when I wanted to throw them out."

He grimaced. "It gets old real fast. You'd think they'd move on from the high-school locker room talk."

She looked skeptical. "You're talking about Buddy Holliday, right? The guy who calls himself Buddy Holly and plays air guitar against his fly?" Sam couldn't prevent a grunt of disgust. Hannah cocked her head and asked casually, "Or is it because they've been betting on a certain doctor over at the hospital?"

Sam folded his arms over his chest and flattened his brows across his forehead. "What are you yapping about now?" Except Hannah wasn't fazed by his intimidating SEAL scowl—in fact, she moved closer, as though anticipating some juicy gossip and didn't want to miss any salacious details. Sam didn't know why she bothered. They could stand at opposite ends of the bar and bellow at each other and no one would hear them over the band.

"Don't worry, Sammy. That lot are big on talk and small on action. Emphasis on small."

"And I need to know this, why?"

Hannah ignored the question. She was like a Rottweiler with a chew toy when she was on the track of something. "Ruben says she could be in Hollywood, playing a classy playboy doctor." She snickered. "I think he's in love."

And suddenly Sam felt like he was suffocating. He tore off his apron and threw it onto the counter behind the bar, barely resisting the urge to rip the bottle of gin out of his sister's hand and smash it into the mirror behind the bar— after emptying the contents down his throat. But he drew the line at sissy drinks and knew his sister would be mad if he broke up the place.

Shoving his fingers through his hair, he bit back an extremely explicit curse. He needed air. He needed to get a grip. He needed to get away from people for a while.

"I'm out of here," he snarled, pushing past his sister. "You're on your own."

Stunned by the leashed violence tightening his face, Hannah turned to gape at him. "Wha—? What did I say? What did I do?"

Sam's snarled expletive over his shoulder died at the baffled hurt in her huge eyes. Guilt slapped at him and he let go with an angry hiss of frustration.

"Nothing," he said, wearily pressing his thumb and forefinger into his eyes to ease the headache threatening to explode his brain, along with his temper. He really needed to get a grip. Hannah didn't deserve his filthy mood. "I'm just tired and I have a headache."

"Again?" She looked concerned. "Do you need to see a doctor?" And all Sam's irritation returned in a rush.

"*No*. I *don't* need to see a damn doctor," he said wearily. "I *am* a doctor, remember?" Her expression turned skeptic and he knew what she was thinking. That he needed a shrink, not an MD.

"You never used to let Buddy bug you, so what's your problem?" she demanded, and before he could remind her he was a SEAL without a team, her eyes got big and a startled laugh escaped. "It's her, isn't it? The fancy Boston doc the guys are always talking about." Her eyes gleamed with fiendish delight, like when she was ten and she'd found him reading the *Playboy* magazine he'd found clearing out Mr. Henderson's garage. He almost expected her to burst out with, "I'm gonna tell Mom." What came out was worse.

"It *is*." She cackled gleefully and before he could ask what the hell she was talking about, she snickered. "*You're* the one with a thing for Doc Boston. Oh, boy, this is great. It's like the time you and Ruben fought over Missy Hawkins, and came home sporting black eyes and split lips. So what's it gonna be, huh? Pistols at dawn or down-'n-dirty street fighting? Can I watch?"

Sam bit back a curse and felt the back of his skull tighten. "And they think *I'm* the family nut job." He squinted at her. "So, what are you, thirteen? I'm a Navy SEAL, for God's sake. We don't get *things* for women or fight over them. People get killed that way."

Hannah's eyes widened, she looked intrigued. "Has that ever happened?"

"*No.*" *Yeesh.* "I don't fight over women. It's juvenile." Not to mention stupidly dangerous.

She stuck her tongue in her cheek. "*R-i-i-ight*," she said, like he was acting so mature.

"Yeah, short stuff. Just remember I know a hundred different ways to kill a man—or a kid sister—that'll look like they died of natural causes. Besides, I'm not interested in some fancy Boston debutante playing wilderness doctor."

Hannah looked disgusted and sent him a *yeah, right* look as she gave his shoulder a patronizing pat. She muttered something that sounded like, "Keep telling yourself that, you poor clueless moron," which he took exception to. But when he demanded she repeat it, she smirked and said, "I've got this, big guy. You go off and crawl into your man cave with your denials and delusions. I'm sure the Navy shrinks will be interested to hear you've finally gone over the edge."

Sam snarled something nasty about Navy shrinks, before turning on his heel and heading down the passage towards the back exit. He yanked open the door and slammed it on the sound of her laughter.

Hannah was wrong, he told himself, firing up the engine and shoving the vehicle into first gear. He *didn't* care if his brother had a "thing" for the fancy doctor. He'd be gone soon and didn't do relationships that lasted more than a week, tops. He was never around long enough for more. And if the voice in his head told him he was deluding himself, he ignored it since it sounded a lot like his sister. He was just tired.

Yeah, he thought with a snort of disgust. He was tired all right. Tired of sitting on his ass, waiting for his CO to call. And he was damn sick and tired of trying to convince people he was fine.

Sam had every intention of heading for the Crash Landing, a rough bar on the other side of town that catered to truckers, loggers and general badasses, but found himself pulling into the hospital parking lot instead.

When he realized where he was, he swore and scowled at the light spilling from the small ER, worried that maybe he *was* as crazy as everyone claimed. Only a crazy man would be sitting outside a hospital, staring at the glowing emergency sign and thinking of a woman whose bedside manner rivaled that of a BUD/S training instructor.

He was also a doctor, for goodness' sake. He could remove his own damn stitches. Nevertheless, he found himself killing the engine and climbing from the cab.

So he was here. Might as well get them removed. They were starting to itch like crazy anyway.

Sam entered the building, surprised to find the reception deserted. He headed for the emergency treatment rooms but found them empty as well. A little alarmed, he retraced his steps just as a door opened somewhere behind him and before he could turn, a voice called out.

"Be right with you… Oh, Samuel, what a surprise," Fran Gilbert, a friend of his mother's, said when she saw him. "Is there a problem?" She was pushing a medicine trolley and looked a little preoccupied. Sam held up his bandaged hand and watched her face clear. "Cassidy will handle that, dear. I'm doing the rounds."

"Busy?"

"Just the usual. In addition to the usual, a dozen pre-schoolers with high fevers came in earlier. We're wait-

ing for spots to appear but in the meantime we've got our
hands full with cranky little people demanding attention
every second. Through that door," she said, gesturing behind him. "I made her take a break. Who knows what will
happen during the night with a bunch of miserable little
people." And then she was gone.

Sam stared after her for a moment, wondering if his
mouth was hanging open. He hadn't had an opportunity to
utter so much as a grunt. Shaking his head, he turned and
headed for the privacy door she'd indicated. He pushed it
open and immediately heard talking.

So much for resting up for a rough night, he thought
darkly. Ignoring the fact that she was free to entertain
whomever she pleased, he let the door shut silently behind
him and headed down the corridor. What he found wiped
all dark thoughts from his head.

Shoving a shoulder against the doorframe, Sam folded
his arms across his chest and let his eyes take a slow jour-
ney up long denim-clad legs perched halfway up a ladder. Doc Boston was alone and muttering to herself about
something that sounded like bedpans and floor polish as
she consulted the clipboard in her hand.

She turned a page to skim it from top to bottom and
then back again, before huffing out a breath and turning
another page, oblivious to his presence.

"You have *got* to be kidding," she muttered with a sound
of disgust. "Who puts bedpans with surgical scrubs? This
system sucks." She froze as though she'd said something
indecent then shook her head with a laugh. "Yes, Cassidy,
you can use the word 'sucks' without the world implod-
ing." She exhaled as she studied the clipboard, her breath
disturbing silvery blonde curls near her face. "Besides, if
someone can walk around with a T-shirt saying '*Eat the
Worm*' or '*Loggers do it with big poles*' in public, you can
certainly say 'sucks' in private without it being followed
by lightning bolts."

Sam grinned. "You sure about that, Doc?" he drawled, making her shriek and jump about a mile into the air. She grabbed for the shelf with one hand and the ladder with the other. The clipboard and pen went flying, her boot slipped and with a panicked shriek she went flying as well.

Without thinking, Sam leapt towards her. She landed against his chest with a thud, knocking the breath from them both. He staggered back against the wall and wrapped one arm securely around her back. The other he clamped around her thighs.

Planting his feet wide to accommodate his curvy armful, he grinned into shocked green eyes, conscious of lush pink lips forming a perfectly round O—which for some reason made him think of hot, wet kisses in the dark—an inch from his.

"I… You… Oh…*God*," she wheezed out, fisting her hand in his T-shirt and sounding about as coherent as Cindy Dawson in the third-grade spelling bee when Frankie Ferguson had let go with a loud burp right there on stage.

She sucked in a shaky breath and uttered one word. "*You!*" Making him wonder if she was relieved to see him or cursing him. He suspected the latter.

"Expecting someone else?" The idea did not appeal.

"I…uh… You…" She shut her mouth with an audible snap and swiped her tongue across her lips. Then, realizing how provocative her action might appear—especially as his gaze had dropped to her mouth—she rolled her eyes and shoved against his chest. "Put me down."

"'I…uh… You'?" Sam lifted his brow, ignoring her order. "You've developed a stutter since I last saw you?"

"*Dammit*, you scared the hell out of me," she snapped, and shoved at his shoulders again.

Both brows hiked up his forehead. "*Hell*?" He was enjoying the feel of her in his arms and the light fruity scent of her hair. He was enjoying seeing her flustered when she was normally so poised. "Doc, Doc, *Doc*," he tutted, shaking his head. "First 'suck' and now 'Dammit' and 'Hell'? What's next? The *b* word?"

Cassidy froze and stared open-mouthed for a couple of beats before a faint flush rose up her neck into her cheeks. "You *heard* all that?" And when his eyes crinkled and his mouth lifted at one corner, she groaned.

"Oh, God, just shoot me."

Sam laughed. "I only shoot bad guys," he assured her, slipping his arm out from under her shapely bottom to let her slide down the length of his body while he enjoyed the friction of soft curves against hard angles. Her face flamed when she felt a certain hard angle and he bit back a groan, suddenly realizing why he'd come.

He wasn't cool with his brother putting the moves on her and he sure as hell didn't like the idea of Buddy or Jake dropping their shorts in her presence either.

Ignoring what that might mean, Sam inhaled the flowery, fresh scent of her hair and enjoyed the soft press of full breasts against his chest. Suddenly nothing mattered but putting his mouth on hers again and finding out if she tasted as good as he remembered.

As if sensing his intent, she made a sound of protest and scrambled out of reach, her eyes huge and dark with suspicion and…was that arousal?

"What are you doing here, Major?" she demanded a little breathlessly. For a long moment he watched from beneath heavy lids before taking a step towards her, enjoying the flash of annoyance that replaced the mild panic when she found herself backed against the wall.

Blocking her escape with a palm to the wall, he tunneled his free hand beneath the soft, fragrant cloud surrounding her flushed face. He wrapped his fingers around the back of her neck and gently pressed his thumb into the soft hollow at the base of her throat. The rapid flutter beneath his touch had him lifting her face to his.

The scent of peaches drifted to him and his gut clenched.

Damn, he thought, *she makes me hungry.* Dropping his gaze to her mouth, he feathered a knuckle across her jaw to the corner of her lips and when her breath hitched in her throat, his blood went hot.

"I had no intention of coming here," he accused in a voice rough and deep with need. "But you…make me crazy. I couldn't stay away."

With a sharply indrawn breath Cassidy fisted her hands in his shirt as though she couldn't make up her mind whether to push him away or pull him close. Sam took advantage of her indecision to open his mouth over hers in a soft kiss that stole her breath and sent his head reeling.

"Samuel," she protested tightly against his mouth.

With a deep "Hmm?" he slid his tongue along her lower lip before dipping inside where she was warm and delicious. He hummed again, this time with growing need.

God, he thought, he hadn't exaggerated the memory of her taste, or the feel of her mouth moving beneath his.

"S-Samuel," she stuttered, "this…this is a bad idea." *You're telling me.* But she didn't pull away, which told Sam he wasn't the only crazy person here. In fact, she tilted her head to give him better access and her breath hitched in her throat.

It was the sign he'd unconsciously been waiting for.

"I like the way you say my name," he growled against her lips, before rocking his mouth over hers, his control rapidly slipping. "I like the way your breath hitches in your throat when you're aroused." He pressed his hips against hers. "It makes me…hard."

"I'm not!" she protested. "I…don't…" Then flattened her palm over his heart, drew in a shaky breath and tried again. "You're *not*." But her words emerged on a moan when she felt exactly how hard he was, ruining her denial.

"I beg to differ," he drawled, and chuckled when she blushed and huffed out an embarrassed giggle.

"No, I'm s-serious," she stuttered, squirming away,

only to find herself backed into a corner. Huffing with annoyance, she narrowed her eyes, stuck out her chin and clenched her hands as though she was contemplating taking a swing at him.

He smiled. He wouldn't mind letting her try.

"Look," she said, shoving the hair off her forehead, "I have bigger problems than your...um, ego, okay?"

Sam folded his arms and propped a shoulder against the wall, taking in the tousled, appealingly flustered picture she made. She looked about sixteen, and there was absolutely nothing cool or distant about Dr. Mahoney from Boston now.

His brow rose. "Yeah, like?" He grinned into her flushed face. "Like why bedpans are listed with surgical scrubs?"

CHAPTER SIX

CASSIDY LAUGHED. "DON'T be ridiculous," she said, rolling her eyes. Her voice had emerged all breathy and excited, like she was a teenager again, for heaven's sake. She'd been muttering about bedpans, of all things, while trying not to think about a certain Navy SEAL. Then suddenly there he was—looking like hot sin, bad attitude and way better than she remembered. And if, when she'd been pressed up against all that hard heat, she'd been tempted to get reacquainted with that awesome body, she wasn't about to admit it out loud. She'd been a little startled, that's all. She was over her attraction to him. Well, mostly.

Looking into his darkly handsome face, Cassidy admitted to herself that he was a very dangerous man. He made her forget about good sense, heartbreak and painful lessons. He made her yearn to toss good sense out with her inhibitions. Fortunately she'd come to her senses in time.

Nibbling nervously on her bottom lip, she kept a wary eye on him and focused on getting her heart rate down from stroke level, only to have it kicking into high gear again when he pushed away from the doorframe.

"Look, Major," she said quickly, throwing up a hand when he moved closer and looked like he wanted to nibble on her lip too. "I'm...busy." His chest connected with her out-flung palm and didn't stop. "*Really* busy." She squeaked and retreated, annoyed that just a minute in his presence and she was acting all girly and flustered. "Stop. *Dammit*, I don't have time for your…um…warped idea of…of foreplay. Samuel, *stop*!"

A dark brow hiked into his hairline and his mouth curled up at one corner. Great, now he was laughing at her. She huffed out a breath. Could this get any more embarrassing?

"Foreplay?"

Ignoring his question and figuring it was rhetorical anyway, Cassidy scuttled sideways and headed for the door, turning when she reached the relative safety of the hallway. *Ready to make a run for it if he made any sudden moves.*

"So what *are* you doing here, Major?" *Besides making my knees wobble and my pulse race.*

He turned, his gaze leisurely moving over her face until his hooded glance met hers, and add making her head spin to his sins. After a long moment, during which Cassidy thought she'd hyperventilate, he finally held up his bandaged hand.

"Oh." Her breath whooshed out and a small frown wrinkled her brow. For heaven's sake, she wasn't disappointed that he hadn't come to push her up against any walls. In fact, she was relieved. She was really very busy and didn't have time for games.

"Why didn't you just say so?" she gritted through clenched teeth, before spinning on her heel to head down the corridor at a sharp clip. She led the way through Reception and into the suture room, reaching for a lab coat on a nearby hook, figuring she needed the added protection against that penetrating gaze if she wanted to appear professional. Heck, if she wanted to *think*.

She fumbled for a button and was horrified to find that her hands were trembling too much to perform a task she'd mastered at five. Biting back a growl of disgust, Cassidy huffed out a breath, smoothed out her expression and turned to find him leaning against the bed, watching her thoughtfully as he slowly unwound the bandage covering his hand.

Crossing her arms beneath her breasts, she made herself focus on medical issues and not on how good he looked. "Frankly, I'm surprised to see you," she remarked, as coolly as if her pulse wasn't skipping all over the place like she was on an adrenaline rush. "I expected you to just rip them out with your teeth."

His raised brow suggested she was missing a few IQ points. "And what?" he demanded. "Use them as lethal spitballs?"

Her lips curled without her permission. "You're exaggerating."

Sam snorted. "Have you ever had nylon thread holding your flesh together?"

"No," she said, taking his hand and feeling the jolt clear to her elbow. *Whoa. Not this again.* Firming her lips, she resolutely ignored the sensation of his warm calloused skin against hers by inspecting the healing wound. After a few moments she reached for needle scissors and gently lifted each suture before snipping and tugging it free. "As a rule I avoid bar fights," she continued, looking up briefly to find his mouth tilted in an ironic half-smile.

Her chest went tight. *Yikes.* The man was living, breathing sin. *And she had a dangerous urge to...well, lick him up one side and down the other.* She frowned at her unprofessional thoughts. "And throwing myself out of moving aircraft."

The chuckle vibrating deep in his chest filled the small room and created an odd sensation in her belly. "You don't know what you're missing."

"Yes, I do," she corrected mildly, as she wiped disinfectant along the tender scar before spraying the area with a thin layer of synthetic skin. "I'm missing broken bones and you're clearly missing your mind." She covered his hand with a waterproof adhesive dressing. "Be careful with that for another few days and keep it clean and dry."

He caught her wrist before she could turn away and her startled gaze rose to his.

"Don't you want to know what it's like…hurtling towards earth at a hundred feet per second?" he murmured deeply, softly.

Cassidy swallowed hard at the expression in his gold eyes. *Holy cow.* "No, I…" *If it's anything like I'm currently feeling…terrifying.*

Without waiting for her brain to clear, Sam reeled her in until the warm male scent of him enveloped her and her common sense scattered, along with her reasons for keeping him at arm's length. In fact, she suddenly couldn't recall why she'd thought this was a bad idea. Without the slightest effort on his part he was rendering her speechless.

"Major…" She thought maybe a token protest was necessary, even though she couldn't remember what she should be protesting against.

"It's like that moment during sex," he rasped, closing the gap to her mouth as she watched, frozen with fascination, "when you realize…" his lips brushed hers and he flattened her captive hand against his chest "…there's no going back."

"Major…" she croaked again, terrified that he would feel the way she trembled. His mouth smiled against hers, as though he knew what he was doing to her. His tongue emerged to sweep across the seam of her mouth. His heart pounded like a jackhammer beneath her palm. *Or was that hers?* "And then, like a heated rush…" he murmured silkily, sending blood thundering in her ears. A breathy whimper escaped and before she could stop it her palm slid up his warm chest to his neck. "It hits you…*wham!*"

She jolted the instant his teeth closed over her bottom lip to tug on the sensitive flesh. Hot shivers scattered from the base of her spine into every cell and Cassidy thought, *Oh, God*, as her knees wobbled.

Before she could protest again, Sam's mouth opened

over hers in a kiss that instantly spiraled out of control. It turned the moisture in her body to steam and sucked air from as far down as her toes.

It felt like she'd been tossed into the center of a tornado. She told herself that if he hadn't been holding her captive she would have pulled away. Broken free. Run for her life.

At least she would have if she'd been able to formulate a single thought. Then she was being yanked up against all his hard heat, his arm an iron band across her back while he fed her hungry kisses that were all tongue and greed and stole her breath along with her mind.

Cassidy's breasts tightened and her blood caught fire. Just when she felt that insidious slide into insanity, he froze and pulled back.

Wha—?

Stunned by the force of emotions storming through her, Cassidy sucked in a desperate breath and stared back at him, wondering a little hysterically if the pounding in her head was a sign that her brain was about to explode. The man literally sucked up everything around him like a level-five twister.

His hands tightened and his eyes looked a little wild—*kind of like she was feeling*—and it took a few moments to realize the pounding wasn't in her head.

A loud *bang* was abruptly followed by yelling that had Sam shifting from sexy and sleepy to sexy and...*lethal*. Without a sound he shoved her roughly aside to move on silent, deadly feet towards the hallway, his hand reaching for...a weapon?

Awareness returned in a rush and Cassidy flung herself after him before he could launch a silent attack on some poor unsuspecting person. She grabbed for his shirt to hold him back and he rounded on her, eyes deadly and cold. It was clearly his attack SEAL face, Cassidy thought with a shudder. She could easily imagine the enemy quailing with terror. Heck, *she* was trembling.

"It's all right, Major, it's just…it's just a medical emergency." At least she hoped it was and not an invasion by paramilitary groups that gossip said hid in the mountains. Then all bets were off. And when he gave no indication that he'd heard, she shook him. "Stand down, Major, I've got this."

For long scary beats he stared at her, his expression cold and flat. Just when she thought he meant to swat her like a pesky fly, he blinked, slowly, like he was coming back from…*a flashback*?

Cassidy gulped, but then his face abruptly lost color and before she could move, he staggered. She reached for him but he threw out a hand to steady himself against the wall.

"Go," he rasped, giving her the sharp edge of his shoulder. She hesitated, watching his forehead drop against the bulge of his biceps. The muscles in his wide back bunched and turned hard. After a couple of hesitant beats she turned and took off down the hallway.

One look at the couple in ER had all thoughts of Sam's flashbacks flying from her head. The woman being propped up by a clearly freaked-out man was as white as a sheet and covered in sweat. She clutched her heavily pregnant belly, and Cassidy noticed blood and fluid staining the front of her maternity dress.

"*Help her,*" the man yelled wildly when he saw Cassidy. "Help her. *Oh, God,* help her. She's bleeding. It won't stop," he croaked pleadingly. "It just won't stop and the baby…" He swallowed. "I think the baby's stuck."

Cassidy grabbed a nearby gurney and met them halfway, swallowing the urge to yell at them for waiting so long. This had all the signs of a home delivery gone wrong. So dreadfully wrong. She just hoped it wasn't too late.

"What happened?" she demanded. "Why didn't you come in earlier?"

"She wanted a home birth, but the midwife's not answering her phone," the man babbled through bloodless lips, his eyes wide and wild. "I didn't know what to do. What the hell do I know about babies? Nothing. I know *nothing… Oh, God,* what have I done?" As white as parchment, he swayed and Cassidy put out a hand to steady him. That's all they needed. Another casualty.

Before she could snap out an order for him to get a grip, the woman gave a low moan and her legs buckled. Yelling out a code blue and hoping someone would hear, Cassidy lurched forward just as the woman fell, her weight taking them both to the floor.

Vaguely aware that the man was screaming and crying hysterically, Cassidy opened her mouth to rap out an order, but the breath had been knocked from her and all she could manage was a strangled gasp.

Sam's face appeared overhead and before she could blink at his abrupt appearance he'd bent and lifted the woman off her with easy strength. Sucking in air, Cassidy scrambled to her feet.

"You okay?" he demanded in a low tone as he gently placed the woman on the gurney.

She should be the one asking but even as she opened her mouth to voice her concerns, she noted that other than a faint pallor and a hard, closed expression, Sam seemed to have recovered. His eyes were clear and sharply focused.

"Cassidy?"

She shook her head to dispel her misgivings and noticed he'd pulled on a lab coat that strained the shoulder seams and rode up his strong wrists. He'd also slung a stethoscope around his neck. He met her pointed look with a raised brow, silently telling her she had more important things to worry about. Things like their distressed patient.

"I'm fine," she rapped out. "Get her details." And took off down the hallway with the gurney, hitting the emergency button as she streaked past.

The next few minutes were a blur as she wheeled the gurney into the OR, where she checked the woman's vitals.

Her concern ratcheted up a notch at the patient's labored breathing and erratic pulse.

"Dammit, dammit, *dammit*," she muttered, grabbing a pair of scissors to cut away the blood-soaked dress. She needed another experienced professional. Preferably someone who had done this before. She needed Dr. Montgomery.

By the time the night nurse burst into the OR, Cassidy had finished intubating the mother. With swift, competent movements she hooked up a saline drip and rapped out orders for drugs.

Ripping open a syringe package with her teeth, she fitted the needle and shoved it into the first vial the nurse handed to her. "Prep her for a C-section," she told the nurse briskly, injecting the contents into the port. "And then call Dr. Montgomery. I'm going to need help on this one."

"You've got help," a deep voice informed her from the doorway and Cassidy looked over her shoulder to see Sam striding into the OR.

Cassidy's eyes widened. "Major—"

"Her name is Gail Sanders," he interrupted in a voice as deep and calm as though he did this every day. "She's a kindergarten teacher. This is her first pregnancy—no history of problems." His eyes were calm and steady on hers. The silent message was clear. They didn't have time to wait for the elderly doctor or discuss *his* mental issues. "Moving her when you're ready."

Cassidy frowned and held his gaze for a couple of beats, conscious of the look of wide-eyed apprehension the nurse flashed between them.

"Dr. Mahoney…?" Heather prompted, breaking the tension filling the room.

"Major Kellan will need the ultrasound,' Cassidy said briskly with a curt nod in Sam's direction, before moving to Gail's feet. They transferred her to the operating table as Heather rolled the ultrasound into position. Cassidy took the proffered tube of gel and squirted a thick line over the apex of the patient's distended belly.

Sam lifted the probe. "Go suit up," he said quietly, eyes on the screen as he rolled the probe through the gel. "I'll handle this."

"Major—" she began, breaking off when his golden eyes lifted. "This is…" She bit her lip and ran her fingers through her hair in agitation. "Are you…?" *Damn.* How did you ask someone if they were sane enough to handle a delicate procedure like this one was going to be?

His face darkened with impatience, and Cassidy knew he wasn't going to discuss what had happened in the hallway. Watching the expert way he wielded the probe, she was forced to admit he looked fine. More than fine. As though he hadn't had a flashback—or whatever had happened—just minutes earlier.

"I'm fine, Doctor," he snapped, returning his attention to the patient. "But *they* aren't and unless you get your ass into gear, they won't be for much longer."

Cassidy hesitated another couple of beats. "I hope you know what you're doing," she said quietly, unsure whom she was addressing.

It took her less than a minute to throw off her clothes, pull on clean scrubs and scrape her hair off her face. By the time she'd finished scrubbing Sam was behind her, holding out a surgical gown that she slipped over her arms after a searching look up into his dark face.

He must have correctly interpreted her probing look because his mouth pulled into a tight line. "This is a job for two people who know what they're doing."

"Monty—"

"Isn't here," he interrupted smoothly. His eyes caught and held hers. "We can't wait, Cassidy. And you know it."

Knowing he was right, Cassidy ground her back molars together. "You're right," she admitted briskly, moving towards the OR doors, "but *you* assist."

Heather Murray had already positioned the colored electrode pads and was fitting a saturation probe over the patient's forefinger when Cassidy hit the doors with her shoulder. Tying the surgical cap at the back of her head, she slipped her hands into surgical gloves the nurse held out.

She watched as Heather hooked Gail up to the heart monitor, a wrinkle of concern marring her brow when a rapid beeping filled the silence. Stepping closer to the ultrasound screen, Cassidy studied the strip of images Sam had printed out, before gently palpating the woman's belly. A quick examination revealed the baby lying breech, with its spine facing upward.

She felt rather than saw Sam come up behind her. "I've delivered babies in worse positions than this," he said at her shoulder.

"So have I," Cassidy agreed, "but not without an OB/GYN on standby. The bleeding is also a major concern." When he remained silent, Cassidy lifted her head to find him studying her intently. Her heart gave a little lurch. "What?"

His eyes lit with a warm smile. "You can do it, Doc. Have a little faith. Besides, I'm right here."

She was about to ask if he'd done *this* before but the monitor beeped and Heather called out, "Heart rate increasing, Doctor," and Cassidy realized they didn't have time to hang around debating his experience.

Sam shoved his hands into latex gloves while the nurse tied his gown and mask. Cassidy moved to the patient's side and hoped she wasn't making a terrible mistake. As the doctor on duty, she was about to trust a man who thought parachuting into hostile territory armed to the teeth was like making love. "Major—" Cassidy began, only to have him cut her off.

"I think we've had this conversation before, *Cassidy*," he drawled, putting her firmly in her place as a colleague now. He looked big and tough and impatient—and most of all competent. After flicking a pointed look at Heather, he returned Cassidy's gaze meaningfully. "We're good."

Biting back a sigh, she opened her mouth and said, "Let's do this."

Heather called anxiously, "Blood pressure dropping, Doctor."

Cassidy's gaze snapped to the monitor. "Keep an eye on the baby's vitals and let me know if Mom's BP drops below fifty." Sam expertly swabbed the woman's belly with iodine as Cassidy waited, scalpel in hand. The instant he was finished she felt for the correct place with her left hand and then made a clean incision with her right. The scalpel sliced through layers of skin, muscle and uterine wall. Sam gently coaxed the baby into position while she slid her hands into the exposed uterus. Within seconds the infant's head and shoulders emerged and Cassidy could see why the baby had been lying breech—and why the mother was bleeding.

The placenta had detached from the uterine wall and the umbilical cord was looped around the baby's neck and under her arm. The infant was blue and flaccid.

Cassidy's heart gave a blip of alarm. *Dammit, dammit, dammit,* she chanted mentally, getting a firm hold on the infant while Sam gently unwound the cord. He accepted the heated towel the nurse offered as Cassidy slid the infant free and handed her over. Deftly cutting the cord, she applied the clip and looked up briefly to catch Sam's intense gaze over the top of his face mask. His gold eyes were dark and solemn on hers. "She's yours," Cassidy said simply, and turned back to save the mother. Gail Sanders's time was running out.

"I've got this," he said, but Cassidy had already tuned out everything, instinct telling her that Sam really *did* have it. She didn't have to make a choice or leave the endangered infant to the nurse.

Besides, there was nothing she could do for the baby now that Sam couldn't do just as well.

Over the next half-hour she communicated with the nurse in terse bursts until she finally managed to get the bleeding under control. Heaving a relieved sigh, she wiped her burning eyes against her shoulder and ordered additional units of blood. Then she set about closing the uterus, the layer of muscle and finally the incision wound.

Lastly, she inserted a drain and stepped back to check the patient's vitals. Finding her still critical but edging toward stable, Cassidy stepped back, wondering for the first time in more than an hour if Sam had managed to save the infant.

She caught sight of him waiting just beyond the lights. For long moments their gazes held, his eyes so intensely gold and solemn her pulse gave a painful little jolt. Had she…? *Oh, God, had she imagined that feeble little cry?* Then his eyes crinkled at the corners in a rare moment of shared accord and gestured to the pink bundle in his arms.

Suddenly tears burned the backs of her eyes and she sucked in a quick breath at the blaze of emotion blocking her throat. *They'd done it,* she thought on a burst of elation that she attributed to their accomplishment and not… well, anything else.

She sent Sam a wobbly smile, rapidly blinking away her emotional tears as she turned back to recheck the patient's vitals to give herself a minute. She clamped off the anesthetic, leaving the shunt in place. "We'll keep her sedated while we wait for the chopper," she told Heather, conscious of Sam's silent scrutiny as they transferred the patient to the gurney.

"You're not keeping her here?" he asked, as they covered Gail with a cotton spread and then a thick woolen blanket. Cassidy shook her head and went to the OR refrigerator, withdrawing a couple of vials of antibiotics.

"The hospital doesn't have the facilities for such a critical patient," she explained, hooking up another saline bag. "Besides, mother and child both need proper neonatal care.

I want them in a large center with access to hi-tech facilities and equipment if anything goes wrong."

Pulling down her face mask, she took a new syringe, slid the needle into first one vial and then the other, finally injecting the cocktail into the new saline bag.

"I'll go speak to her husband," she said, when she finally ran out of things to do, her emotions suddenly as fragile as the lives they'd just saved.

Disposing of needle, syringe and surgical gloves, she quickly wrote down the details of the procedure and the drugs she'd used. With a sigh of relief she turned to leave, stiffening in surprise when long fingers closed over her shoulder.

Looking up into Sam's shadowed face, Cassidy sucked in a startled breath. Illumination from the surgical lights slid across the bottom half of his face, leaving the rest in deep shadow. It made him appear bigger and darker and… *hell*, more dangerous than ever.

Unbidden, images of what had happened in the suture room flashed through her head and she winced. *Darn*. One look into his dark gold eyes brought on a flashback of his mouth closing over hers in a hot, greedy kiss. She'd hoped to escape before he remembered that she'd almost climbed into his lap and rubbed her body against his. She licked dry lips.

"What?" she asked huskily, her throat tight with awkwardness and a sudden baffling anxiety.

"You want to see her?"

Sam watched confusion chase wariness across Cassidy's face until he gently handed over his precious bundle. She'd been instrumental in saving the infant and deserved to share the joy of that new life.

Drawn by the subtle scent of her, easily discernible even over the antiseptic smells of the OR, Sam moved closer. He'd been immensely impressed with her ability and the efficient way she'd handled the crisis. She'd never once hesitated or panicked. Hell, he'd seen seasoned soldiers panic in less dire situations and had to admire how she'd kept a cool head.

It had been touch and go there for a while, but the newborn was finally pink and glowing with life. Tiny hands were tucked against a petal-soft cheek and the infant looked, Sam thought, like a cherub praying. Huge dark eyes stared up into Cassidy's face with such mesmerizing intensity that the hair on his arms and the back of his neck rose. It was as though she knew she was being held by someone...special.

Her expression both delighted and enthralled, Cassidy gently touched a pink cheek and the tiny folded hands. "Look, Sam," she breathed, "she looks like a little angel. Like she's praying. Isn't she the most beautiful thing you've ever seen?"

For long silent moments Sam found his gaze locked on Cassidy's face, unable to utter a sound. Her expression was one he'd never thought to see on her beautiful face—soft and sweet and glowing with uncomplicated delight.

God, he thought painfully, *she really is beautiful.* And so much more than he'd thought. Swallowing the lump blocking his vocal cords, he finally managed a raspy, "Yeah. Beautiful."

Oblivious to his chaotic emotions, she continued to murmur softly to the infant, laughing when the little rosebud mouth opened in a wide yawn.

Feeling like he'd been shot in the chest with a high-powered rifle, Sam forced his emotions under control and moved to untie her gown. He finally gave in to the urge to brush his lips against the long elegant line of her throat as he leaned forward to murmur, "You did great, Doc."

Goose bumps broke out across her skin and a shiver moved through her as she jerked away, her face flushing as she aimed an uncertain smile in his direction. At least he wasn't alone in this unwanted attraction, he thought with satisfaction.

"You too, Major," she answered briskly, carefully avoiding touching him as she passed the infant back. She moved away jerkily, looking suddenly tired—and spooked, like she was ready to bolt.

He tucked the baby into the crook of his arm. "Cassidy?"

She paused in the process of pulling off the surgical gown and sent him a look over her shoulder, eyes wide and a little desperate.

"Yes?"

"You going to finish what you started earlier...before we were interrupted?"

Immediately a wild flush heated her face and her eyes widened as though she thought he was suggesting they finish their interrupted kiss. Her mouth opened but all that emerged was a strangled, "Uh..."

"I have another twenty-seven stitches," he went on, grinning wickedly at the deer-in-the-headlights expression that flashed across her face. Her mouth closed with a snap and her look of furious embarrassment had his soft chuckle following in her wake.

"Meet me in the ER in fifteen minutes," she snapped, and Sam got the impression she'd considered punching the smile off his face. He was suddenly glad he was holding a newborn.

Cassidy Mahoney, it seemed, was not a woman to be trifled with. And why that made his grin widen, he didn't know. Maybe he was an idiot, or crazy, like his family believed.

"What do you think?" he asked the infant staring intently up at him. The tiny girl blinked before surrendering to another big yawn, making Sam chuckle.

"Yeah," he snorted softly, "my thoughts exactly, sweetheart."

CHAPTER SEVEN

CASSIDY SENT FRAN GILBERT to the ER to deal with a hot, appealing SEAL, assuring herself she wasn't a coward. Besides, Gail's husband needed a status update.

She found Chip Sanders being fussed over by one of the older nurses on duty. The warm, motherly woman in her late fifties squeezed the new father's hand in silent support when they caught sight of Cassidy heading in their direction.

His expression was so painfully hopeful that Cassidy had to smile in reassurance as she announced that he had a beautiful baby daughter and that his wife's progress was promising.

Chip leapt up with a joyous whoop and Cassidy had to laugh when he caught her in a huge grateful hug. She briefly returned his embrace, cautioning that Gail was still critical and that she and the baby were being transferred to Spruce Ridge General.

After he rushed off to see his new family, she found herself smiling as she headed for the wards. There was nothing like making someone so happy they forgot all trauma and fear, she mused. Fortunately for Chip, everything had worked out fine.

Thanks to one overwhelming Navy SEAL. A man who seemed to have a really bad effect on her. Just the sound of his deep voice sent excited little zings into places that had no business zinging and she ended up losing a good portion of her brain.

Just as Cassidy was writing notations on the night roster, news came through that the chopper was five minutes out. After giving the night nurse a few last-minute instructions, Cassidy headed for Recovery to collect the patients for transport.

She...*they* had done everything they could to ensure Gail Sanders and her baby pulled through the traumatic incident. It was now up to the OB/GYN at Spruce Ridge General to ensure they stayed that way.

Heather was waiting for her and together they rushed the new family to the helipad, where the Medevac helicopter was already landing. While the paramedics transferred Gail and her baby to the chopper, Cassidy gave the Medevac doctor a rundown of the patient's condition and signed the release forms. With a nod, the guy sent her an appreciative smile and an over-the-shoulder thumbs-up as he loped off towards the waiting craft. Bare minutes after it had landed, the chopper was heading towards Spruce Ridge.

Beside her, Heather gave a huge sigh and sent Cassidy an elated smile. "Wasn't that just great? I love it when a bad situation turns out well, don't you?" She threw her arms around Cassidy and made her laugh with an exuberant hug. "Ooh, and wasn't the major just wonderful? With Gail's baby, I mean," she added hastily, when Cassidy drew back with a dry look. "I heard Chip was blubbering like a little girl," Heather chatted on. "Poor guy. He must have been terrified." She stopped to sigh dramatically. "Isn't he just dreamy?"

Cassidy eyed her sharply. "Who? Chip?"

Heather giggled. "No, silly. Samuel Kellan. Just wait until I tell the girls what happened. They're going to flip. Imagine, me getting to see him in action with my own eyes?" She squeaked and gave Cassidy another quick hug.

Then with a hurried, "You're the greatest, Doc," she turned and disappeared into the darkened hospital.

Cassidy shook her head at the departing nurse and turned to watch as the chopper's running lights rose over the dark mountains. With the *whup, whup, whup* fading into the night, she took deep breaths of cold mountain air and slowly let the tension of the night slide away.

"Well," she said dryly to no one in particular, "it seems Crescent Lake's hero has done it again."

She wasn't jealous that Major Hotstuff was getting all the credit for the night's work, she assured herself. He'd stepped up when she'd needed him, it was true, but you'd think he'd performed a miracle worthy of sainthood.

Laughing at herself, Cassidy went to tell Fran she was taking a break. Hoping to get a few hours' sleep before the next emergency, she headed for the quiet of her office.

The privacy hallway connecting the offices was in darkness but dim light eased its way through an open doorway. Cassidy's pulse gave a little bump and she paused as the scene brought back unpleasant memories. Fear clutched at her belly until she reminded herself that Crescent Lake wasn't Boston. Drugged-up vice cops didn't break into doctors' offices in small mountain towns, looking for prescription drugs. At least she hoped not.

Besides, in the few weeks she'd been in town the most dangerous thing to happen had been when she'd been escorted to the local jail to treat a hot, attitude-ridden Navy SEAL.

No, that wasn't quite true, she amended silently. *That* had been when he'd pushed her up against the ER wall and rearranged her brain synapses.

Heart hammering, Cassidy quietly approached the open doorway. She drew in a wobbly breath and peered around the door, half expecting to find crazed druggies ripping open drawers looking for their next fix. Her breath escaped in a whoosh when she found everything as it should be.

She was sliding her hand up the wall to turn off the light when she realized the desk lamp was on and not the ceiling fixture. Heading across the room, she reached over the desk to extinguish the lamp when a soft sound had her wide gaze flying towards the shadows. The sight of Crescent Lake's favorite son draped over the sofa with an arm flung across his face, gave her a weird sense of déjà vu.

Straightening, Cassidy allowed her hand to fall away. It seemed the man couldn't find anything big enough to accommodate his large body. She wondered absently why he hadn't left, and took the opportunity to study him without him being aware.

He was back in the faded jeans and she took a moment to admire the way the soft material hugged his narrow hips and long muscular legs while cupping more intimate places. The black T-shirt fitted even more snugly, stretching across his wide chest while straining the shoulder seams and the sleeves around his big biceps.

It was only when she could see his lashes casting dark shadows on the slash of his cheekbones that she realized she'd moved across the room and was standing staring down at him like an infatuated adolescent.

Darn, she thought, biting her lip, getting all excited about some *guy* was the height of idiocy—especially one who liked free-falling from high altitudes and blowing stuff up. One who wouldn't be sticking around for long before he was off again, saving the world.

Turning to go, she spied a blanket over the back of the sofa and reached for it an instant before hard fingers clamped over her wrist. In less time than it took for her heart to jerk hard against her ribs, she was flying through the air to land with a bone-rattling thud that knocked the air from her lungs. She barely managed a strangled *oomph* as a heavy weight rolled her across the floor.

They came to an abrupt stop against the solid desk with

Cassidy's wrists shackled over her head. A large hand clamped over her mouth, stifling her shocked gasp.

Blinking, Cassidy found herself staring up into a dark face lit with fierce gold eyes. For an awful moment she visualized him whipping out a knife and slicing her throat before she could draw her next breath.

She felt him everywhere—heat and hardness pressing her soft curves into the floor. During the tumble, one long, hard thigh had found its way between hers, effectively pinning her down. All she could do was gasp and stare into gleaming gold eyes as she waited for his next move.

One second she could see her life flashing before her eyes, the next he was cursing and rolling away to lie silently and rigidly beside her. The suddenness of the move stunned her and all she could do was try to calm her jagged pulse and smooth her ragged breathing. All she could think was, *What the heck was that?* It had been scary and…*darn it*…she hated to admit it a little exciting.

She was a sick person.

She felt rather than saw his head turn. "You okay?"

And he was insane.

Sucking in air, Cassidy lowered her arms and pushed her hair off her face before rearing upright to glare down at him.

"Are you insane?" she demanded furiously, then snapped her mouth closed when she realized that maybe it wasn't the most sensitive thing to say to someone suffering from PTSD—if that's what he had—but, *heck*, the man gave being trigger-happy a bad name.

Not surprisingly, he didn't look the least bit amused by what had happened. In fact, he looked mad—well, that made two of them—and embarrassed.

Embarrassed? What did he *have to be embarrassed about?* She *was the one who'd gone flying through the air.*

He scrubbed a hand over his face with a weary sigh and growled, "Sorry…" so softly she almost didn't catch it.

Her jaw dropped open. "Sorry? You're...*sorry*?" She was getting hysterical again and made an effort to lower her voice, even though she felt she was entitled to a little hysteria. "You can't attack people like that and just say sorry, Major."

He turned and scowled, his dark brows flattening across his forehead in a heavy line of frustration. "What the hell do you expect me to say? Besides, it was your fault."

Her eyebrows shot into her hairline. "*My f-fault?*" she spluttered, and when he smirked she had to get a firm grip on her temper before she gave in to the urge to smack it off his face.

"Hey, you were bending over me," he pointed out reasonably, as if he had women bending over him all the time. And after witnessing Heather's gushing infatuation, he probably did. *The jerk.* "What was I supposed to think? I thought you wanted to wrestle me to the floor. I was just being accommodating."

Cassidy stared at him open-mouthed for a few seconds as his words sank in then uttered a sound of disbelief. She drew up her legs and shoved her hands in her hair before dropping her forehead onto her knees. She snickered helplessly for a few beats. "You are such a liar," she said when she could talk without gasping.

He lifted the arm he'd slung over his face to crinkle his eyes at her, his poet's mouth pulled into a crooked smile. *God, that little grin was appealing.*

"Says who? *You?*" He made a rude sound. "For all I know, you *were* just looking for an excuse to roll around on the floor with me. *You* know, finish what you started earlier?"

"What *you* started, you mean," she retorted.

"Me?" He shook his head. "You have a defective memory there, Doc."

"And you're delusional. I ought to throw you out." Another mocking sound accompanied the *yeah-right* look he sent her and she narrowed her gaze. "You don't think I can?"

"Babe, I *know* you can't."

He sounded so arrogantly male that she straightened and stared at him. "Excuse me," she demanded frostily. "Did you just call me *babe*?"

He grinned and said, "Uh-huh," with the kind of look that had a bubble of laughter rising in her throat. *Darn*. She didn't want to find him irresistible, but there was just too much to like. Despite…well, everything.

Blowing out a breath, she dropped her head back against the desk, suddenly exhausted by her ping-ponging emotions. "Well, don't. It's demeaning."

"It is?" He sounded genuinely surprised. "Why?"

Cassidy snorted. "You ask that when you probably call every woman you meet *babe* because it saves you having to remember their names."

Sam was quiet for a moment, as though he was seriously considering her accusation, before finally shaking his head and saying, "That's not true. I don't call the ward sergeant at Coronado Med Center *babe*." He gave a shudder. "*Or* my CO's wife, for that matter. That's a surefire way for a guy to get court-martialed."

Cassidy caught herself smiling when she couldn't afford to. He was too big, too macho, too…*everything*. Everything she'd told herself she didn't want in a man. Everything she was finding alarmingly likeable.

She pushed out her lower lip and blew out a frustrated breath. "You're changing the subject, Major. It isn't normal for anyone to think they're being attacked in their sleep. I was just reaching for the blanket."

"That's what you say," he said, waggling his eyebrows at her when she rolled her eyes. Snagging her wrist, he tugged her towards him, tucking her body beneath his when she lost her balance. Cassidy once again found herself staring up into his darkly handsome face while his big body covered hers.

"What are you *doing*?" she squeaked, realizing his hard thigh was pressing against places that hadn't seen any action in a long while. It was mortifying to admit those places were turning liquid with heat.

"If you need to ask," Sam said, sliding his hand over her hip to rub his thumb into the crease her jeans created between hip and thigh, "you're not as smart as I thought."

She slapped a hand over his to stop him heading for forbidden territory. "I'm smart enough to know that whatever you're thinking is a mistake."

"*This*," he murmured, and dropped a kiss at the outer corner of her eyebrow, "is not a mistake." He slid his mouth to her ear. "SEALs carry really big weapons," he whispered wickedly. "Wanna see?"

Cassidy's gasp ended on a giggle at his terrible pun. *Yes, please.* "No!" She groaned silently. *No looking at his… weapon.* Or anything else.

"Major," she began, trying to sound firm, but her voice gave a little hitch as arousal sent heat skittering through her veins. "Let me up." If she stayed spread out beneath him like jelly on peanut butter, there was no telling what would happen.

His eyes had gone all dark and hot. He shook his head slowly. "I can't," he confessed, abruptly serious. Catching her hand, he brought it to his mouth, where he pressed a gentle kiss into the center of her palm. "I've tried. *God* knows, I've tried." He nibbled on the fleshy part of her thumb. "There's just no denying…*this*."

Her belly tightened and she let her fingers curl helplessly over his jaw, rough with a dark shadow that looked a good few hours past five o'clock. The rasp against her skin sent shivers of longing and arousal up her arm into her chest and a hot yearning set up residence in her belly. "Try harder," she gulped.

His smile was quick and sinful as his big hand smoothed a path of heat down the length of her arm, over her shoulder to her breast. "*Babe*," he drawled, brushing his thumb over the full bottom curve and drawing her nipple into a tight bud that had his eyes gleaming with satisfaction. "If it gets any harder I'll injure myself." He looked up from studying the hard tips of her breasts. "You're bound by oath to treat me then, aren't you?"

Cassidy slapped her hand over his with the intention of moving it to safer territory. "In your dreams, Major," she scoffed huskily, but her resistance was fast slipping away— right along with her mind. And she was having a hard time recalling why she should care.

"Sam," he corrected against her throat, and Cassidy lifted her chin to give him room, her eyes drifting closed with the lush pleasure of having his mouth on her. *Oh, God.* They needed to stop this before…before…

"Say it." A shiver raced down her spine, sparks bursting behind her eyelids as he opened his mouth to suck on a patch of delicate skin. She gave a little gasp and clenched her thighs around his, the pressure setting off tiny little explosions of sensation in forbidden places.

"Wh-what?" She tried to concentrate long enough to make sense of his words.

"My name." He abandoned her throat to kiss his way up to her parted lips. His thigh pushed harder against her. "Say it," he ordered softly, pulling back when she tried to capture his mouth with hers. A moan worked its way up from her throat and emerged as a growl before she could stop it. Tunneling her fingers into his hair, she tugged him closer and closed her teeth over his bottom lip in a punishing little nip.

"Don't make me hurt you, Major," she growled, and his answering chuckle was deep and dark and sent delicious sensations heating up lonely places. *Heck*, he was like a furnace, incinerating everything in sight—her resistance, her reservations…her *mind*—turning her to putty in his big, strong hands.

His mouth smiled against hers. "Say it," he taunted softly, applying a little hot, wet suction that made her moan. "Say it and I'll give you exactly what you want."

Cassidy heard a loud buzzing in her ears and in a far distant corner of her mind still capable of thought she acknowledged that he was right. She did want him and his name, "*Samuel,*" emerged on a husky sigh.

With a growl, deep and low in his throat, he caught her mouth in a kiss so hot and raw that she felt it in the pit of her belly. He pulled oxygen from her lungs and a frantic response from her mouth. It was so good that Cassidy fisted her hands in his hair and opened her mouth beneath his, promising herself that she would stop. In a minute.

It was her last rational thought. The instant his warm hand slid over the naked skin of her belly, she lost all reason, all ability to think of anything but the sudden frenzy of his kiss. Excited thrills raced over her skin as her world narrowed and focused on his hot mouth, his eager hands. She tried to touch him everywhere at once—his shoulders, his wide back, his hard chest—as though she couldn't get enough.

She briefly acknowledged that she was in trouble—*big* trouble—when his hand slid beneath her jeans and cupped her through her panties. Thought slid away on a low moan as she arched into his touch, feeling perhaps for the first time the kind of hot, crazy desire people talked about. Too far gone to care that he was everything that was bad for her.

His touch felt too good, and the big erection pressing against her felt hard and powerful and welcome.

He shifted and before she knew it, he was whipping her T-shirt over her head. Grabbing a fistful of fabric at the back of his neck, he stripped off his own, sending both garments sailing over his shoulder into the shadows. Then he planted his big hands beside her head, and with their gazes locked he nudged her thighs apart before lowering his body slowly over hers until all that separated their good parts was denim and silk. At the press of his powerful erection into the notch between her legs he grimaced as though in pain and his eyes drifted closed.

"*Jeez*," he said, his voice so deep and rough it slid into her belly like dark sin. "*Cassidy...*" he breathed heavily, and stared down into her face with hot, glazed eyes. "You are so damn beautiful, do you know that? And I've had really carnal thoughts about your mouth for days," he growled. "It's driven me crazy, thinking about kissing you. Kind of like this." He bent his head and gave her a kiss, soft and sweet and hot. "*Oh, yeah*," he breathed against her mouth, sucking gently on her swollen lip. "It's lush and tempting and so damn sweet. It's all I can think about."

Then he opened his mouth over hers in a hard, hungry kiss that scattered her senses, and before Cassidy knew what was happening she was thrusting her hands into his hair and kissing him back, her mouth as hot and greedy as his.

Sam swept his tongue past her lips to taste the dark, sweet nectar within. She responded with a low hungry moan and closed her lips around his tongue, sucking hard.

Controlling himself with effort, Sam fed her hot, desperate kisses, tongue dueling and tangling while his hands streaked over her soft flesh, stripping off her clothing until she was left in nothing but a tiny triangle of teal silk.

Kneeing her smooth thighs apart, he settled his hips between them, pushing against her soft, wet heat until she was writhing restlessly against him.

"*Holy...*" His mind glazed over and he couldn't remember what he'd been about to say. Only knew that he wanted her more than he'd wanted anything. *Ever*.

"Samuel..." Her voice was a sweet, husky moan of desire that almost had him going off like a missile. He filled his big hands with her breasts and flicked at the hard little buds until a long, low wail tore from her throat and her back arched up off the floor.

Ignoring her entreaty, he dipped his head to scrape his teeth along her neck, nipping the delicate skin until she shivered as her palm slid down his belly. She pressed her hand against his button fly and he jolted like he'd been shot.

"*Sweet...*" he growled, grabbing her hand to pin it against the floor above her head. "Not yet, babe." He gave a rough laugh when a sound of frustration burst from her mouth. "Soon," he promised hoarsely, closing his mouth hungrily over one swollen breast. She gasped and his pulse spiked until all he could hear in the quiet room was the heavy thunder of his heart, the harsh sounds of their breathing and her soft, throaty whimpers.

She fisted her free hand in his hair and couldn't hold back the full-body shudder or the eager moan that ended with, "*Oh, my God...*"

Soothing her, he dropped a moist kiss between her lush breasts before heading south, stringing tiny, wet kisses across her abdomen. He paused to trace his tongue around her shallow navel, gently blowing against the damp skin until her belly quivered. His hum of amusement turned into a growl of pleasure.

With his mouth on her flat belly, Sam slid his hands up her long smooth thigh to hook his fingers into the narrow band of fabric at her hips. And before she could gasp out a breathless "*Wait,*" he'd slid her panties down her legs and past her toes to send them sailing over his shoulder.

Grunting, he reared back onto his heels and looked at the woman sprawled like sin before him. For a moment he savored the tempting sight then dipped his head to run the tip of his tongue up the inside of her knee, chuckling when she shivered and let out a desperate whimper.

As though sensing the direction of his mouth, Cassidy uttered a squeak of protest and tried to clamp her legs together, fisting her hands in his hair to stop his upward progress. "No, Samuel," she cried breathlessly, "I don't—"

"It's okay," he murmured, sliding his big, rough hand over her quivering belly before wedging his shoulders between her thighs. He dragged damp kisses over her hips and stomach to the soft, sweet undersides of her breasts. Alternating stinging wet kisses with little swipes of his beard-roughened jaw that made her arch and moan, Sam gentled her with his hands and lips until her muscles went fluid and lax and she gave a long, lazy hum of pleasure.

The moment he felt her body shift languorously and turn liquid he moved and closed his mouth over her soft, damp folds. She tried to tug at him, her gasp of protest turning to a cry of pleasure as he pressed closer and did something with his tongue. In moments she was flying off the edge.

The force of her climax hit hard, and, eyes wide with shock, Cassidy could only lie there shuddering and think, *Holy cow...what was that?*

But Sam wasn't finished. He uttered a rough growl and reared up, yanking his jeans and boxer briefs down his legs before kicking them free. Then he slid up her body, dragging his tongue along the slick, damp flesh between her breasts and up her long slender throat until his fallen-angel face filled her vision. His molten-gold eyes locked with hers. She felt the bump of him against the tender flesh between her thighs and slapped a hand against his chest to keep him from thrusting home.

"Condom," she gasped.

He froze and swore, surging upward to reach behind him for his jeans. Within seconds he'd rolled the latex down his thick shaft before he positioned himself and, with one fierce thrust, buried himself deep.

The thick, solid invasion set off another series of explosions, sending Cassidy arching upward as her body stretched to accommodate him. It took a couple of thrusts but once he was buried to the hilt she let out a long low moan of pleasure and wrapped her arms and legs around his big body.

Softly murmuring her name, Sam slowly withdrew until she was lightheaded with the incredible explosion of sensations. Then he thrust deeper, his mouth closing over hers in a ravenous kiss that stole her breath and blew away what was left of her mind.

Applying the same light suction to her mouth that he'd used in more intimate places, Sam sucked the air from her lungs until she was dizzy, mindless with pleasure. Then he began to move in a slow, sweet rhythm. The sensations shooting through her ratcheted higher and higher until her blood caught fire and her world spun off its axis.

Before she knew it, she was straining against him, meeting his every hard thrust with one of her own, tongues tangling and clashing as her hands raced over him, greedy for the feel of his hot, tight flesh and the steel-hard muscles shifting and bunching beneath the smooth damp skin.

Helpless with sensation, Cassidy sank her fingers into his big shoulders and clung, her third climax catching her completely unawares as it ripped a low moan from her throat. Her body bucked and convulsed beneath his, the soft growl in her ear scraping at raw nerve endings and sending more detonations exploding through her blood.

Catching her hips in his hands, Sam dug his fingers into the smooth flesh to hold her in place as he increased his pace until he was hammering every hard inch, every powerful thrust into her as though he wanted to stamp his possession onto her very DNA.

Caught up in his desperate pace, Cassidy wrapped her long legs around him, and fisting her hands in his hair was lost to his driving rhythm. Hard and fast—plunging into her deeper and deeper—until, with a hoarse cry, he came.

CHAPTER EIGHT

THE BAD THING about disastrous mistakes was that no matter how hard you tried not to think about them, the more you did. It was this vicious cycle that gave Cassidy a headache and made her cranky in the week following…well, possibly the second-biggest mistake of her life. And even if she'd managed to forget for an instant that she'd had a one-night stand with someone so completely wrong for her, she just had to catch sight of her reflection and she was groaning in mortification.

Crescent Lake's favorite son had whipped her up, given her some seriously intense orgasms and when she'd thought he was sleeping and had tried to sneak away—they had been in someone's office, for heaven's sake—he'd tightened his hold on her and said in his deep sleep-rough voice, "Where are you going? I've just started."

Even hours later her skin glowed, her eyes sparkled and her mouth was bruised and swollen from his kisses. Anyone looking at her could see at a glance that she'd had her world rocked. And if that wasn't enough, she had whisker burns and hickeys in places that made her alternately smile and blush.

Except there was absolutely *nothing* to smile about. She'd rolled around on the floor—*and* the huge sofa—with a hot Navy SEAL whose idea of a relationship probably meant a couple of nights with a busty babe before he headed off to wreak havoc in some foreign war zone.

What had she been thinking?

Clearly she hadn't given a thought to where they were or the consequences of someone walking in on them. The last thing she wanted was to find herself hip-deep in another scandal. The last thing she needed was to get all worked up over some hot alpha SEAL with "temporary" tattooed on his sexy hide in eleven different languages.

Clearly the smartest thing to do was escape. Except every time she'd tried to slide out from under his big arm, he'd tightened his grasp, his sleep-rough voice murmuring, "I'm not finished with you yet."

Finally her brain had cleared and she'd told him she needed to check the wards. His heavy arm had reluctantly slid away but not before a big rough hand had smoothed a leisurely line of fire from her naked shoulder to her knee and he'd murmured, "Hurry back…" against her throat.

Resisting the urge to arch into his touch and purr with pleasure, Cassidy had rolled off the sofa, snatched up her clothes and bolted. Standing in the shower an hour later, she'd leaned her forehead against the tiles as steaming water had cascaded over her sensitized flesh and prayed that he'd be recalled to wherever he was stationed. Because there was no way she could ever look into his wicked eyes and not remember where he'd put his mouth and how he'd done things that had made her scream.

Okay, maybe not scream, she amended, but she'd made some pretty embarrassing noises that had her blushing whenever she thought about it. But as the days passed and the gossip mill in town had him harassing bad guys and helping little old ladies across the street—when he wasn't working behind the bar and chatting up the regulars—Cassidy realized he wasn't going anywhere. *Yet.*

And when the thought of him leaving made her feel

vaguely ill and a strange ache squeezed her chest, Cassidy began to get a very bad feeling that unless she got her head on straight, she was headed for heartbreak. Besides, he hadn't called or tried to contact her, which clearly meant he was done with her.

And she was done too—*really*. So why, then, did his absence feel like a slap in the face?

But that kind of thinking was not only ridiculous but self-defeating. Samuel Kellan had "temporary" written all over him and what had seemed like more than hot steamy sex—at least to her—had been nothing but a good time for him,

In the week since he'd toppled her to the floor and brought her intimate places out of deep hibernation, he hadn't been there to rescue her from falling off ladders or to push her up against any walls. And as she left the hospital eight days later and slid into her car, she firmly told herself she was relieved. She didn't need rescuing. And she didn't need a big, strong man with a wicked smile to rock her world.

Considering what she'd endured the past year she'd be really, *really* stupid to fall for another alpha male—even one with beautiful gold eyes, awesome biceps and the ability to reduce her to a mindless mess.

Except her confusion and uncertainty grew, along with the sick feeling that her emotions were deeper than she wanted to acknowledge, and that what she'd dubbed "just sex" had been anything but.

Frankly the smart thing was to pretend nothing had happened and wait for the churning in her belly to go away. Besides, there hadn't been time to develop deep lasting feelings for someone like him.

That would have been so utterly stupid when she'd already used up her quota of stupid on a man who lived on the edge.

* * *

The following week found Sam riding shotgun while Crescent Lake's sheriff droned on and on about something or other till Sam had been tempted to drive them both off a cliff. So he'd been a bit bad-tempered. *Big deal.* Instead of doing the job the government was paying him to do, he was driving around looking for truant kids and mediating between two old codgers who'd been fighting like toddlers over a toy truck for *fifty* years. And if that wasn't bad enough, the lean, mean badass SEAL had been dumped after the best sex of his life.

Okay, so maybe a *very* small part of his surliness was because he'd thought Cassidy Mahoney would be as eager as he was for a repeat of their night of passion. Instead, she'd escaped at the first opportunity. And all he'd done since then was think about her.

Like a damn girl—obsessing about what she was doing, who she was with and if she thought about him at all. Frankly, he was behaving like a pimply-faced nerd with his first crush. She'd slid her perfect body against his, put her lush mouth and her hands on him and made his eyes roll back in his head. Then she'd calmly risen from the sofa, collected her clothes and sauntered from the room without a backward glance.

Maybe in the past he'd encouraged it, but he really hated it that Cassidy had done it to him. Maybe it made him a hypocrite, but there was just something about her that made Sam lose his mind and act like a lovesick ass. It was baffling—and downright terrifying.

So he told himself to stay away. He was leaving and had no place in his life for the kind of relationship she probably wanted. His life was perfect…except he had to listen to Ruben go on and on about seeing a shrink so Sam could get back to protecting the nation because he was giving the sheriff's department a bad name by being a jerk.

And in the next breath he was telling Sam how great it

would be if he came home so they could run the department together.

Yeah, right. Like that would ever happen. Ruben liked being in charge and so did he. They would probably throttle each other in the first week.

Sam sighed—again—and wiped the already clean bar surface. Fortunately it was Sunday night and the bar was quiet except for a few die-hard regulars huddled in booths along the wall, and Sam didn't have to exert himself making conversation. Except it gave him way too much time to think—which was something he wanted to avoid like a tax audit.

The truth was he was bored. Bored with driving around harassing people during the day, only to serve them Buds and peanuts at night. So when his brother pushed through the front doors, Sam was ready to take his frustrations out on someone.

"I don't know who called you but I haven't beaten anyone up lately," he drawled, folding his arms across his chest and eyeing his brother darkly. "But I could always make an exception with you."

"No one called to complain," Sheriff Kellan said tiredly. "At least, not in the last three hours."

"Real funny. Beer?"

"God, yeah." Ruben pulled off his hat and tossed it onto the bar counter. He slid onto a stool and ran a hand through his hair. "I'm off duty. Sort of."

"How can you be 'sort of' off duty?" Sam demanded, sliding a bottle across the counter.

"I'm not here to hold up the bar and swap life stories with the barman," Ruben said tiredly, lifting the beer to his mouth.

"That's a good thing," Sam snorted. "I already know your life story, and it's about as exciting as a visit to the dentist. If you've come to nag me about my crappy attitude again I'm going to have to physically remove you."

Ruben smirked and lifted his brow in that superior big-brother way that used to drive Sam crazy as a kid. "*Right*," he snorted, and lifted the bottle in an ironic salute. "Like I'd let you." He took a couple of deep pulls before lowering the bottle an inch and fixing Sam with his dark gaze. "Got a job for you."

"In case you haven't noticed," Sam complained, "I already have a job. Hell, *three* if you count driving around in an air-conditioned SUV harassing innocent folk all day and serving beer to snarky sheriffs at night. You can do your own damn filing. Besides, I have to sleep some time."

Ruben snorted since they both knew Sam wasn't getting a lot of sleep. "Marty and Andy are back at work tomorrow and I'm tired of keeping you out of trouble. It's exhausting. Besides, with your attitude you're not exactly cut out for the sheriff's department."

Sam sent him a mocking look. "Just this morning you were telling me I should come home and join you fighting the terrible crime in Crescent Lake," he drawled. "Make up your mind."

Ruben shook his head. "Don't know what I was thinking."

"What changed your mind?"

"I need your unique skills."

Sam lifted an eyebrow. "You want me to kill someone? Blow something up? Infiltrate enemy territory?" He tutted and shook his head. "This from the man sworn to uphold the law."

"Not those skills, you moron. I'm talking about the medical degree you acquired on the taxpayer's dime. I need a doctor."

Sam arched his brow sardonically. "You sick? Your girlfriend find out she's pregnant with quadruplets?"

An irritated look crossed Ruben's face. "No, I'm not sick. And when do I have time to date?"

Sam shrugged, unconcerned with his brother's love life.

"How should I know? Most days you're so busy nagging I can't wait to get away from you. Besides, the idea of discussing your sex life is just disturbing. I don't want those visuals in my head. I have enough nightmares."

"Yeah, well, I'd like to have a sex life but I'm too busy protecting the innocent people of Crescent Lake from moody badass SEALs. Besides, I have a problem only you can solve. I just got off the phone. Doc Monty was run off the road up in Spruce Ridge. They had to cut him from his car and now he's in County Gen with concussion and a shattered hip."

"*Holy...* Is he all right?"

Ruben sighed and scrubbed a hand down his face. "I think so. Anyway, we need a doctor. Like now."

"In case you've forgotten, you already have a doctor. The one from Boston? The one Hannah says you have a thing for?"

Ruben's eyes glinted and his mouth turned up in a smirk that Sam was sorely tempted to remove. Ruben shrugged. "Well, she's beautiful, single and doesn't hold up bar counters in Spruce County. What more could a guy want?" He took a drink. "In fact, I was thinking of going over to the inn later and telling her about Old Monty. Maybe ask her out." And when Sam growled a warning low in his throat, Ruben snickered. "Maybe even stay the night." Then he burst out laughing. "*Jeez,*" he gasped when he finally caught his breath, "you should see your face."

Sam folded his arms across his chest and narrowed his eyes, barely resisting the urge to reach across the bar and punch someone.

"You *do* remember I've been trained by the government to kill scum like you, don't you?" he drawled dryly, but that only made Ruben laugh even more until he was laughing so hard people from the booths in the back were craning their necks to see what was happening.

Sam ignored them and shook his head with disgust. "You're pathetic, you know that?"

Finally Ruben wiped his eyes and took a drink of beer. "No more than you," he snorted with a wide grin. "It's like you're sixteen again and mooning over Cheryl Ungemeyer."

"I did not *moon* over Cheryl. I was temporarily…um… distracted by her endowments. Especially the summer she wore that string bikini. I was young and impressionable and she was an older woman." He paused a couple of beats. "I'm neither young nor impressionable now."

"Cheryl's small fry compared to Doc Boston," Ruben told him, waggling his eyebrows. "Any idiot can see that."

"You keep your eyes, and everything else, off her endowments," Sam warned half-heartedly, pointing a finger at his brother. He knew Ruben was just yanking his chain, but it wouldn't hurt to warn the guy off. "She's a doctor, for goodness' sake."

Ruben shorted with disgust. "You should listen to yourself," he said, before finishing his beer in a couple long swallows. He set the empty bottle on the bar and rose. "I guess I'll have to look around for another medic, then," he said with an exaggerated sigh. "Maybe that guy from Redfern. The nurses all had a thing for him last time he helped out."

Sam snarled and reached over the bar to grab his brother's shirt. He yanked him close until they were nose to nose, before saying mildly, "You do that and you're a dead man." He let Ruben go with a shove. "Tell Doc Boston I'll see her in the morning."

Ruben laughed and smoothed the front of his shirt before reaching for his sheriff's hat. "Tell her yourself, stud," he said, slapping it onto his head as he turned to saunter from the bar, leaving Sam with the nasty suspicion he'd just been played.

* * *

It was past ten when a quiet knock at the door distracted Cassidy from the article she'd been reading about surgical procedures for head trauma patients. All very cutting edge and fascinating but she was having trouble concentrating.

Wondering who on earth could be visiting her at such a late hour, she tossed the journal aside and rose from the rumpled bed to pad across the floor to the door.

Expecting to see the innkeeper, she was unnerved to find a US Navy SEAL propping up the door frame, hands shoved into jeans pockets, radiating enough virility and attitude to give a woman bad ideas. Ideas she should be done with.

The shoulders of his jacket were damp and rain dotted his dark, ruffled hair. His eyes and most of his face were shadowed, leaving his left cheekbone and half his mouth and strong jaw illuminated by the hallway light.

Heat rose in her cheeks as his hooded gaze boldly swept from the top of her tousled hair to her bare feet. Her grip tightening on the door, Cassidy barely resisted the urge to slam it in his face or—worse—cover her breasts. And since he'd already seen every inch of her naked body, that, and slamming the door, would only make her look ridiculous.

It was the first time she'd seen him since he'd rocked her world and she couldn't help being conscious of her nudity beneath the thin tank top and long track pants she wore as pajamas.

"Major," she said coolly in greeting. A dark brow rose at her tone and his mouth kicked up at one corner.

"Doctor," he mocked, and after a few beats, during which he continued to study her silently, Cassidy gave in to the urge to flick her tongue nervously over her lips. His eyes went hot at the move.

Finally, when she could no longer stand the rising tension, she demanded, "What are you doing here, Major?"

"Invite me in and I'll tell you."

Wary of his strange mood, Cassidy eyed him suspiciously. "Why can't you tell me out here?"

A slow, wicked smile curved his mouth. "You want the entire floor to hear what I have to say, *babe*?"

Flushing at his reminder of the night they'd spent together, she narrowed her eyes and fought the urge to slam the door in his face-even if it did make her look like an idiot. He must have read her mind because he pushed away from the wall and stepped into her, forcing her back into the room to avoid coming into contact with his hard heat.

"Come in, why don't you?" she drawled dryly.

"Why, thank you, Dr. Honey," he mocked softly, "don't mind if I do." He angled his shoulders, intentionally brushing against her as he moved past. A shiver of awareness spread across her skin, tightening her breasts. Cassidy retreated while Sam continued into the room then turned to lean back against the door, hoping it would support her wobbly knees.

He simply took over her space with his presence, leaving Cassidy fighting twin urges to plaster herself against him or run like hell.

He shrugged off his battered leather jacket and tossed it over the back of an armchair, clearly intent on staying a while. She eyed the way his dark blue T-shirt molded to wide shoulders and a strong back and her hands tingled at the memory of running them over hard muscles covered with warm, satin-smooth skin.

Thrusting his hands on his narrow hips, Sam took his time looking around the room, making Cassidy painfully aware of her rumpled appearance and the large bed dominating the space. Glowing bedside lamps gave the room an intimate glow that had her recalling in perfect detail the last time they'd been in a room together.

He turned, catching her gaze over one broad shoulder. The hot, sleepy expression in his eyes told her his thoughts were moving along similar lines.

"You bailed." He sounded vaguely accusing, which surprised her since she'd thought they'd both wanted to avoid any "after" awkwardness. Talking about it now was not only redundant, it was…mortifying. She wanted to forget the whole incident. But if he wanted to discuss it, the least she could do was be honest.

"Look, Major, I'm not looking to start…well, anything. It…it was a mistake," she finished firmly.

His eyes darkened and his jaw flexed. "A mistake?"

Suddenly parched, she pushed away from the door and headed for the small bar fridge, determined not to let him distract her with memories of "the sofa interlude." It was over and she wasn't going there again.

She bent at the waist to grab a bottle of water and looked over her shoulder, only to catch his smoldering gaze on her backside. She straightened with a snap and "Can I get you something?" emerged on a breathless little squeak.

Unconcerned that he'd been caught ogling, Sam's brooding gaze traveled up the length of her body until his eyes met hers, heat and accusation in his expression. He shook his head. "I'm good."

Yeah, right.

She headed for the window with her bottle, hoping a little distance would help her breathe in the suddenly hot, airless room. She turned and propped her hip against the windowsill. "Why are you here, Major?" she demanded, twisting off the cap. "Are you ill? Find out your girlfriend has an STD?"

His lips twitched but he shook his head slowly, eyes scorching and intense as he watched her lift the bottle and drink thirstily. He licked his lips, his gaze travelling from her mouth, down her throat to her tight breasts. He didn't look sick, she thought a little wildly. In fact, he looked fabulous. And hot. *Dammit.*

"Is something…um wrong?" she asked hoarsely, before

clearing her throat irritably. "*Do* you need a doctor?" Her gaze checked him for blood and found none.

"Yes… No." He moved across the floor and her heart skipped a few too many beats when he came to a halt less than a foot away. His gold eyes studied her as though he'd never seen her before. "*You* do."

"I—what?" *What the heck was he talking about?*

"Monty had an accident on his way back from visiting his daughter. He's in Spruce Ridge General."

Cassidy gasped and felt her face drain of color. She tightened her hand on the plastic bottle. "Oh, God, is he all right?" She hadn't known the older man long but had come to like and respect him enormously.

"Shattered hip. He'll be out of commission for a while."

"You know as well as I do that he won't be back," she told him quietly. "After something like that the workload would likely kill him. Besides, he should be enjoying his retirement."

"He's been treating people here for the past forty-five years. Hell, he *is* the hospital."

"He still needs to enjoy his retirement."

"Tell that to him. Besides, Crescent Lake's tourism has soared over the past five years. The hospital needs someone younger who can cope with the workload." He paused. "So. You interested?"

Cassidy's heart skipped a beat but she knew enough not to read too much into his question. He wasn't asking because *he* wanted her to stay. "What about you?"

He sent her an impatient look. "I already have a job," he reminded her shortly.

"Yes," she agreed shortly. "Yelling '*boo-yah*' as you jump from high altitudes."

"That's right." His brows lowered and he folded his arms across his chest. "You make it sound like a kids' game."

"No, it's not and I appreciate that you risk your life with

every mission, but you're more than a SEAL, Major. You're more than infiltration, interrogation and demolition."

"Yeah," he agreed silky. "I'm damn good at my job."

"You'd have to be. But you can't be a SEAL for ever."

A dark brow rose arrogantly. "I can't?"

Rolling her eyes, Cassidy recapped the water bottle with an irritated twist. "You know you can't," she said flatly, slapping the bottle on the windowsill with a snap. He caught and held her gaze with an intensity she felt like a burn in her gut. "Eventually you have to retire or move up the ladder."

"Or come home in a body bag."

"Don't say that," she snapped, suddenly furious with his dry flippancy. The thought of him being KIA made her queasy. She gulped, pushing her hair off her forehead with unsteady fingers. "*God*, don't say that. Just…just…*don't*."

"Every soldier, every sailor thinks about it," he reminded her gently. "It's the reality of being in any country's armed forces. *Hell*, before every mission we write letters to our families and get our affairs in order."

Cassidy felt tears burning the backs of her eyes, pressure squeezing her chest like a vice. She pressed the heels of her hands against her eyes to counteract the sudden threat of tears. "That's… *Dammit*. That's not fair."

A slow, satisfied smile lit his dark features. "Sounds like you care what happens to me," he said cockily, the masculine confidence in his voice sending her belly dipping and her temper rising. She wanted to simultaneously slug him and wrap her arms around him.

"Of course I care," she snapped hotly, before realizing how he might interpret her words. "You're…you're a valuable member of the country's special armed forces. I'd care about anyone I knew going off to fight a dangerous war."

His looked skeptical. "*Riiiiight.*" He stepped closer to plant his big boots either side of her bare feet and slapped both hands on the windowsill at her hips, effectively boxing her in. Then he leant down to brush his lips against the delicate skin beneath her ear.

"Are you sure you wouldn't miss me?" he demanded softly.

Cassidy gulped and her head spun with the warm, male scent of him. "I…uh."

"Not even a little?" he whispered, giving her earlobe a tiny nip that sent shivers of pure sensation spreading throughout her body. The back of her neck prickled, her breasts tightened and familiar heat pooled between her thighs. And when his mouth opened against her throat she moaned, tilting her head to the side to give him room. She wanted to beg him to stop one instant and the next—

"Samuel." Her voice emerged, husky and aching with a desire she could no longer deny. She wanted him. Needed the hot slide of his flesh against hers more than she needed her next breath. "This is a mistake."

"No," he rasped against her neck. "Inevitable."

She gave a breathless moan when his hands curled around her knees, pushed them gently apart to step between them until his heat and hardness pressed against where she ached.

"Admit it," he insisted softly, his hands smoothing a line of fire up her thighs to her hips. "Admit that you'd miss me if some scumbag terrorist took me out," he said against her mouth.

Dizzy with the force of her emotions, Cassidy slid her palms up his long muscular arms to his shoulders and fought the urge to clutch him close. She wondered briefly why she'd imagined she could ignore him, especially when he touched her like this. Put his mouth on her. Talked about dying.

"Yes," she breathed against his mouth, sliding her hands into his thick hair. "*God, yes*," and caught his mouth in a kiss that showed him exactly how much she would miss him. How much she'd come to need him despite her determination not to.

Sam growled deep in his throat and lifted her, yanking her hard against him. And when her legs snaked around his hips, he turned towards the rumpled bed.

"Show me, Cassidy," he growled against her throat. "Show me how much you'd miss me."

CHAPTER NINE

WHEN CASSIDY WOKE the following morning she was naked and aching in deliciously intimate places. *Again*.

Only this time *she* was alone and didn't have to scramble around looking for her clothes.

Sliding her hand over the bed where Sam's big body had heated up the sheets, she told herself she was relieved. But the truth was the hollow feeling in her chest made her feel like a hypocrite.

In the dark, intimate hours of the night she'd pressed her body to his, arched into his hungry caresses and moaned when he'd moved his hot, moist mouth over every inch of skin and thrust his body into hers. And when their ragged, harsh breathing had calmed and their skin cooled, he'd pulled her close and wrapped his arms around her as she'd slid bonelessly into sleep.

As if he'd never let her go.

He'd made her feel safe and protected as she hadn't felt in a long time—as though within his arms she'd found her shelter from the storm.

Which was ridiculous.

Samuel J. Kellan *was* the storm. He'd blown into her life when she'd been determined to hide from the world. He'd turned her inside out with his sexy smile and hot, seductive kisses that made her feel—things she didn't want to feel—and then he'd given her a glimpse of the caring, honorable man beneath the tough, broody SEAL exterior. *Worst* of all he'd made her admire him when she'd been convinced he was exactly like Lance Turnbull.

Okay, so she liked him too—a *lot*—but that was beside the point. He'd soon be back with his team, plotting mayhem and destruction in the world's hottest hotspots and she'd be…here. A world away.

Her one-night stand had just become two, and she didn't know what that meant, how she felt about it or if she wanted more. Heck, if *he* wanted more.

Fortunately, by the time she walked into the hospital she'd managed to get her wildly unstable emotions under control. Until she saw *him*—tall and darkly handsome—surrounded by animated adoring women and looking like a large hungry predator in a hen house.

As though his senses were attuned to her, Sam's head lifted and his eyes met hers across the room. The force of his gaze hit her like a sledgehammer, leaving Cassidy stunned and gasping for air because that look said he saw things she'd rather keep hidden. Things that had become painfully obvious last night when he'd talked about dying. Things she'd refused to acknowledge. Even to herself. *Oh, God.* Even with the truth staring her in the face.

Then his eyes crinkled in a private, evocative smile meant to remind her of hot, wet mouths and frantic, greedy hands. Her heart lurched in her chest before taking off like a crazed meth head fleeing from the cops.

Shocked and a little spooked by her reaction, she turned and hurried towards the hallway leading to her office, her palm hitting the door as though she couldn't escape fast enough. In reality she wanted to run for the exit and keep going until the feelings faded. But she had an awful feeling she couldn't run too far or too fast. Everything that had happened with Sam was burned indelibly into her mind—*heck*, her soul—and running would accomplish nothing.

Besides, she wasn't the kind of woman who got swept away by a couple of nights with a sexy Navy SEAL.

Was she?

Hyperventilating and angry with herself for making more of things than they were, Cassidy stormed into her office and yanked off her jacket. She flung it at the coat rack and tossed her purse into her bottom drawer with shaking hands, then gave the drawer a frustrated little kick.

What the hell was that?

"What the hell was that?"

Cassidy froze when the low, furious demand filled the room. A frisson of alarm skated up her spine as memories roared in of the last time she'd been cornered in an office by an angry man. Drawing in a steadying breath, she gathered her professionalism around her like an invisible cloak and turned to find him looking hot and annoyed and more than a little baffled.

Sam wasn't Lance, she reminded herself. And he wasn't a desperate, drug-crazed psycho.

"Excuse me?" she asked coolly, hoping he'd take the hint and back the hell off. With her emotions frayed and ragged, she wasn't up to a confrontation without exposing emotions scraped raw from panic.

Sam folded his arms across his chest, his dark brows a slash of irritation across the bridge of his nose. "You heard me."

Cassidy lifted her chin in challenge. "What was what?" She had the satisfaction of seeing a muscle twitch in his jaw. *Good,* she thought uncharitably, *I'm not the only unhinged person here.*

"*That,*" he snapped, pointing at her. "In here. Out there. It's like you're two different people. It's confusing as hell. I never know where I am with you."

All thoughts of poise and cool professionalism forgotten, Cassidy stared back at him frostily and ignored the way her stomach clenched. "I don't know what you're talking about."

"*Jeez,* Cassidy," he said roughly, his face harsh with some fierce emotion he seemed to be struggling with. "One minute you're all warm and sweet and sexy and the next… hell, you looked at me like I'm the Greenside rapist."

Wincing inwardly, Cassidy turned away, hunching her shoulders against the truth. She smoothed unsteady hands down her thighs. "You're imagining things. I was just a little surprised to see you, that's all. I'm—" She stopped abruptly when she turned to find him a couple inches away. Her eyes widened and she uttered an audible gasp. *Yikes.* The man moved like smoke.

She gulped and backed up a step. He was so close, so… *familiar.*

"That's bull."

"I beg your pardon?"

"You heard me," he growled, his deep voice scraping against ragged nerve endings. "I'm not some muscle-bound redneck you can intimidate with the frosty debutante routine."

Staring into eyes fierce with a confusing mix of emotions, Cassidy swallowed past the lump in her throat and sighed. "It's…complicated." She shrugged helplessly. "Just old, not-so-pleasant memories. Ancient history. Really."

After a long moment he lifted a hand and brushed his knuckles across her jaw. Surprise at the gentle touch added to her ragged emotions. Emotions she didn't want or need. Emotions that made her feel fragile and susceptible and long for something she couldn't have.

"Wanna talk about it?"

A strangled laugh escaped and she finally found the strength to move away from the temptation to lean on him, draw in some of his strength and heat.

"*God, no.* It's nothing, *really.*" She drew in a fortifying breath and turned, eager to change the subject. "So, what *are* you doing here?"

His gaze narrowed, probed. "I told you last night."

"You *did*?" Now it was Cassidy's turn to be confused.

"Yeah. I told you Monty had an accident and the mayor asked me to fill in until they can get someone else—or I'm recalled." He gave a one-shouldered shrug. "Whichever comes first."

Cassidy frowned as though trying to recall what he'd said last night. "You told me about the accident." She remembered him talking about body bags and dying and then— "You never said anything about filling in as medic," she added quickly, memories of what had followed flooding her with heat. *Yeesh. So not the time to be thinking about that.* "I would have remembered."

Sam eyed her flushed face silently for a few beats then his mouth slowly curved into a smartass grin that she wanted to simultaneously smack and kiss. "You thought I was here to take up where we left off last night, didn't you?"

She flushed. "Of course not," she denied instantly, smoothing her already smooth French twist with shaking hands. "That's…that's insane," she finished lamely, trying to hide her shock at discovering they would be working closely together. *Oh, boy.*

"You *did*." His grin faded into a harsh frown and his mouth twisted. She could feel him withdrawing. "I think I get it now. Negative reaction, ancient history. I reminded you of some scumbag stalker, didn't I?" Without waiting for a response, he swore and shoved his fingers through his hair. "What the hell kind of man do you take me for?"

"Th-that's ridiculous," she spluttered and turned to reach for the clean lab coat hanging on the back of her chair to give her hands something to do. "Why would I th-think that?" Large, warm hands dropped onto her shoulders and she tensed, abruptly sucking in a shaky breath.

"Hey." His voice, deep and rough, slid inside her chest

and aimed for her heart. "Is that what you think?" he demanded hoarsely. "That I would…hell…*could* hurt you?"

Cassidy looked up over her shoulder into his face and couldn't deny the sincerity behind the baffled hurt and anger. Sighing, she made herself relax and ignored the temptation to lean back against him, let him wrap his arms around her. Like he had during the night. But she couldn't. He might say he wouldn't hurt her, but he would. Not intentionally or physically. She didn't think he was capable of that. But he most definitely would hurt her. And soon.

"No, I don't," she denied, easing out from beneath his hands and moving a safe distance away. *Not really.* "A year ago I made the mistake of trusting…well, someone I shouldn't have."

She felt him come up behind her. "What happened?"

Cassidy sighed, admitting to herself that he deserved to know why she behaved like she had a multiple personality. "Lance is…*was* a vice cop. Charming, handsome…" Her mouth twisted wryly. "A hero. He…um…he was brought into ER after a drug bust went wrong."

"I sense that's not the only thing that went wrong."

Cassidy flushed with embarrassment, hating that she'd been so naïve. "He came to thank me for saving his life. An exaggeration, but he was sweet and…well—"

"Charming?" Sam demanded darkly, and when she remained silent he cursed softly. "And you fell for it."

Cassidy gritted her teeth. "I guess you could say that."

"But?"

"He had a habit of seducing women in the medical profession."

"Let me guess. He liked all the attention?" He sounded disgusted.

Cassidy shrugged. "That too."

"There's more?"

"He stole my security card and helped himself to the dispensary."

"*Holy cr*—! He stole drugs?"

"For which I was blamed. The cops were called in. Fortunately for me he was already under investigation and my testimony…well, suffice it to say he's no longer a cop."

"Good for you. I hope the bastard rots in jail." He was silent a moment. "You were exonerated?"

"Yes, but…"

"Again *but*?"

"Things got…well, *difficult* after that."

"They fired you?" He sounded outraged.

She shook her head. "No. But sometimes I think it might have been better if they had. There was a lot of gossip and jokes. Cruel jokes." She shrugged. "You know what it's like in hospitals. So…I eventually resigned and moved here." Cassidy abruptly became all business. "As I said, Major, ancient history."

A dark brow hiked up his forehead at her cool tone and his eyes darkened. "Are we back to that, *Doctor*?"

Cassidy sighed. "Look, last night was a—"

"Don't say it," he interrupted her shortly, taking a couple of long strides in her direction. Her eyes widened and she quickly moved to put the desk between them. He halted, shoving his hands on his narrow hips as he studied her, brows lowered in visible frustration.

"It *was* a mistake," she insisted, resisting the urge to roll her eyes since "mistake" was a major understatement. At least for her it was. It meant she could no longer blame her behavior on adrenaline. But he would still leave, and if she let her feelings develop, what then?

Sam was silent for so long she began to rearrange her desk to give her hands something to do. Just when she thought he'd finally taken the hint and left, a large hand covered hers.

She froze, staring down at the sight of her pale, slender hand engulfed in his. His hand was huge, tanned and broad with long skilled fingers that were capable of killing a man, bringing a baby back from the brink of death—and driving a woman out of her mind with pleasure.

The strength of it should have scared her but for some strange reason it just felt…right. *He* felt right. As though her hand had been fashioned to fit perfectly into his.

But that was a dangerous illusion and one she needed to get out of her head. He wasn't perfect, she reminded herself firmly. He was fighting demons as hard as he fought for his country. The combination wasn't healthy. For either of them.

"Why?" he demanded softly. "You didn't have a good time?"

Making a sound in her throat that was a cross between a laugh and groan, Cassidy stopped trying to escape and looked up over her shoulder into his fallen-angel face. She would like to say no, but she couldn't lie to him, not any more. So she said instead, "I refuse to answer that on the grounds that it may incriminate me."

Sam used his grasp on her hand to whip her around and tug her against him. "Then what's the problem?" His free arm snaked around her waist and his lips brushed her temple.

Cassidy pressed her palms against the hard heat of his chest and fought the urge to slide them up to cup his firm jaw, tunnel into his thick dark hair. "You. Me… Hell, I don't know. I just know it can't happen again."

His arms tightened as though he would pull her into him. "Why not?" He sounded baffled and frustrated. "You had a good time and I sure as hell did."

Cassidy sighed and pressed her face wearily into his throat, tempted to close her eyes and burrow deep. Until she absorbed his heat, his strength. Or he absorbed all of her.

"Lots of reasons," she murmured, drinking in his clean masculine smell. "One of which is that we're now working together. I don't sleep with colleagues."

"Glad to hear it," he drawled, smoothing a hand down

her back to her hip to press her closer. "I would have really hated punching Monty's lights out."

Cassidy grimaced and pushed away from him, feeling off balance like she'd entered an episode of *some adventure game show* dressed in a designer suit and four-inch heels. "That's disgusting."

"Besides, neither of us is married." He paused as though a horrible thought just occurred to him. "Are you?"

Cassidy gaped at him. "No!"

He shrugged but looked ridiculously relieved. "Then what's wrong with enjoying each other?"

"While you're here, you mean?"

He frowned and leaned back so he could look into her face. "Is that a problem?"

Sighing, Cassidy told herself she wasn't disappointed. She'd known from the beginning she was nothing more than a temporary distraction.

"I'm not built for temporary, Sam, and everything about you says your bags are packed and all you need is one phone call."

His hands dropped and she could see the truth in his eyes. Her heart squeezed, though she didn't know what she'd expected him to say. Deny it maybe?

Fortunately a voice from the doorway stopped her from humiliating herself further.

"Cassidy, Mrs. West is... Oh." Janice paused as if she sensed the tension in the room. "I'm sorry," she said, her eyes wide and curious. "I didn't realize you were busy."

"We're not," Cassidy said briskly, reaching out to snag the stethoscope she'd tossed onto the desk the previous night. "I was just on my way. Is Mrs. West in exam room one?"

"Yes, Doctor," the nurse said, wide eyes bouncing between Cassidy and Sam. "Hank Dougherty is waiting in two."

"Thank you, Janice," Cassidy said, looping the stetho-

scope around her neck. "I'll be right there. In the meantime, can you please hunt up a lab coat for Major Kellan and
inform the staff that he's filling in for Dr. Montgomery?"

Janice beamed at Sam, and Cassidy could practically
hear the woman's heart go pitter-pat. "I heard." Janice
grinned excitedly. "Welcome aboard," she gushed.

And giggled when his "Thanks" was accompanied by
a crooked grin.

Taking that as her cue, Cassidy headed for the door,
desperate to escape before he remembered what they'd
been discussing. His voice, dark as midnight and rough
as crushed velvet, reached across the room and stopped
her in her tracks. "I'm not him, Cassidy," he called softly,
and her fingers tightened on the doorframe. She chanced
a look across her shoulder.

"Not who?" she asked past the lump of yearning in her
throat. A yearning she didn't want to analyze too closely.

"I'm not what's-his-name? Lance Full-of-bull."

"Today is senior citizen clinic day," she said briskly instead of replying to what was largely rhetorical anyway.
"Hank Dougherty needs hip replacement surgery but he
needs to get his smoking under control first. Don't let the
old codger con you into thinking he's quit."

Removing the stethoscope from her ears, Cassidy smiled
reassuringly at the anxious young mother hovering close.
"Chest is all clear," she announced, "but this little butter-
ball has a bad fever and her ears are inflamed."

She reached for a tongue depressor. "Open your mouth
wide, sweetie," she cajoled gently, "I want to check if the
bad germs got into your throat."

The child gazed back with huge, tragic eyes and held
out the stuffed toy she was clutching. "Elmo first," she
rasped, looking on intently as Cassidy examined Elmo's
throat and made some doctor noises. "Do you think you
and Elmo have the same bad germs?" Cassidy asked, hold-

ing out a new depressor. The little girl nodded and obedi-
ently opened her mouth.

"Uh-oh," she said, with an exaggerated look of dismay.
"Just as I thought. Have you two been sharing a toothbrush
again?" Jenny giggled around the thumb she'd instantly
shoved in her mouth and shook her head. "That's good
because Elmo needs his own toothbrush." She tapped a
little button nose and lifted the child into her arms. "And
you need to suck on something other than that thumb. How
about a magic lollipop?"

"Magic?" Jenny rasped shyly around her thumb.

"Uh-huh. One that'll chase away all those bad germs,"
Cassidy explained, reaching into a nearby cabinet. "And
make your throat feel better." She held out two antibacte-
rial lollipops. "There," she said, handing the little girl to her
mother. "One for you and one for Elmo." Returning to her
desk, she slid a handful of M&Ms into a small clear plastic
bag and wrote "Elmo" in permanent marker on the front.

"This is for Elmo but your mommy's going to have to
get your medication from the pharmacy," she explained
to the wide-eyed child. "Elmo is pretty bad at taking his
medicine. I want you to be a big girl and show him how
it's done. Can you do that for me?"

Jenny nodded solemnly as her mother smiled at Cassidy.
"Thank you so much, Dr. Mahoney. You're really good with
children," she said. "Are you a pediatrician?"

Cassidy shook her head. "I specialized in ER medicine.
And it's Cassidy."

"Thank you, Cassidy. And welcome to Crescent Lake."

Smiling, Cassidy sent the child a little wave over her
mother's shoulder as the two left her office, and had only
a couple of minutes to gulp down rapidly cooling coffee
before her next appointment arrived.

A clearly harassed Cathy Howard entered with a rowdy,
tow-headed toddler and sank wearily into the nearest chair.
Little Timmy Howard had been one of her first patients.

"Did I ever say I wanted him bouncing around again?" Cathy asked Cassidy with a grimace. "I would give *anything* for just *one* minute of peace."

Cassidy rounded her desk and looked into Timmy's big blue eyes, catching the wicked sparkle that would one day drive girls wild. Grinning, she swooped on him before he could escape, and plopped him down on the bed.

She laughed as he tried to wriggle free. "Come here, you little monkey. I want to listen to the engine inside your chest and see if all your spots have gone."

Timmy gurgled and pulled up his shirt, exposing his little pot belly. "See," he said, tucking his chin onto his chest and peering down at his tummy. "Gone."

"Are you sure?" Cassidy sounded dubious. "I think I see one here." She tickled him, making him squirm and chortle. "And here?" The noisy raspberry she blew on his tummy made him squeal and try to squirm away, but she held him firmly. "What about here?" He gave a great big belly laugh and caught her face in his hands before planting a big wet kiss on her nose.

Cassidy laughed and brushed white-blond curls off his face. "I bet you do that to all the girls," she teased, lifting him onto his sturdy little legs. He wrapped his chubby arms around her neck and bounced happily while she listened to his chest. Satisfied that he had no after-effects of the virus, she lifted him into her arms.

Turning to hand him to his mother, she came face to face with Sam. Her heart jolted and she sucked in a startled breath. They hadn't been this close since she'd told him she couldn't get involved with him.

"Oh. Major Kellan, you...you startled me."

"You got a minute, Doc?"

Belatedly noting his shuttered expression and the grim set of his mouth, Cassidy felt a prickle of alarm. A quick examination revealed blood staining the gray T-shirt beneath his lab coat and her skin went ice cold.

"Samuel—?"

"You finished up here?" he interrupted, flashing a quick look over her shoulder at the room's occupant. "Hey, Cath," he greeted the other woman with a quick smile of familiarity. "How's Frank?"

"Hi, Sam," Cathy Howard greeted him back, her eyes alight with avid curiosity. "He's great. Thanks for asking."

"You need to come with me," he said to Cassidy, lowering his voice and backing into the hallway. "*Now.*"

Dropping a quick kiss on Timmy's curls, she handed him to his mother. "Cathy, Timmy seems fine," she told the other woman, her attention on Sam's tense back. "If you're worried about anything, don't hesitate to bring him in. Keep him quiet for another day or two and be sure to give him a multivitamin and plenty of fluids."

She murmured a hasty goodbye and hurried after Sam, calling out to Janice at Reception that they had a code blue. Fortunately it was the midafternoon lull and she was certain Fran could handle the few patients that remained.

Cassidy hurriedly caught up to Sam, her pulse a blip of anxiety as she searched for injuries.

"Where are you hurt?"

His black brows came together over the bridge of his nose. "What?"

She drew level with him and gestured to his gray T-shirt and jeans. "Blood. Where are you hurt?"

He frowned down at himself. "It's not mine. A logger's just been brought in. Bad weather caused a cable to snap. He was in the way."

"Where is he?"

"OR. I can handle it if you're busy."

Almost running to keep up with his long strides, she sent him a sideways glance. "Fran's got the clinic. What's his condition?"

A muscle jumped in his jaw. His short reply, "Bad," sent an icy chill skating down her spine.

A white-faced Jim Bowen was already lying on the operating table, his shirt and jacket wet with his blood. Heather
Murray was at his side, holding a pressure bandage over
the wound, while a middle-aged man held his shoulders
and talked quietly to him. Another younger man hovered
nearby, looking like he was on the verge of passing out.
His relief when he saw Sam turned to confusion when he
spotted Cassidy.

"I thought you were getting the doctor?"

Sam's brow lifted and he sent Cassidy a wry smile. "I
did," he drawled. "This is Dr. Mahoney. She's an ER specialist from Boston."

Ignoring the skepticism in the young man's eyes, Cassidy moved towards the patient, noting his gray-tinged skin.
She lifted her head and caught Sam's gaze. "Heather, could
you please show the gentlemen out and get Spruce Ridge
on standby. Major Kellan and I will handle this until you
return."

Cassidy barely noticed the men leaving as she quickly
shed her lab coat and pulled on a surgical gown. Tossing another to Sam, she liberally sprayed her hands and arms with
disinfectant before grabbing two pairs of surgical gloves
from a nearby dispenser. She shoved her hands into one
pair and waited while Sam disinfected. There wasn't time
to scrub.

With swift, economical moves, Cassidy cut Jim's shirt
away while Sam inserted the stent and hooked up a saline
drip. For several minutes they worked together in silence,
cleaning the patient's chest and arm, positioning electrode
disks and hooking him up to the heart monitor.

Cassidy clipped on the saturation probe and frowned as
thready, irregular pulse beats blipped into the silence. Jim
had clearly lost a lot of blood and was going into shock.

"He's going to need an orthopedic specialist," Sam said,
tying Cassidy's face mask and shoving her hair under the

surgical cap as she gently eased pressure on the dressing to assess the extent of the damage.

Jim's arm had almost been severed at the shoulder and the instant she released the pressure, blood gushed from the jagged wound. "Can't wait," she said briskly, reaching for a clamp. "We're going to have to repair this artery first or he won't make the orthopod."

"Heather," she said briskly when the nurse returned, "find out his blood type and get the status with Spruce Ridge changed to code blue. What's our blood status? He's going to need at least six units."

"Four in total," Sam said from the refrigerator, "and they're all O positive."

They shared a look and Cassidy made a split-second decision she hoped she wouldn't regret. "We'll use them all and substitute the rest with blood plasma."

Sam's brow rose up his forehead. "And if he's AB negative?"

"We'll cross that bridge when we come to it."

CHAPTER TEN

Cassidy stared in dismay at the ominous storm front that had rolled over the mountains while she and Sam had been in the OR. And if that wasn't bad enough, the helicopter pilot presently running towards them was alone. He wasn't even Medevac. A Forestry Services chopper had responded to their emergency.

Just great.

"Where's the Medevac crew?" she yelled, pushing her whipping hair off her face. The icy wind roaring down the mountain held more than a hint of snow and she had a feeling the storm was closing fast.

"You're it," he yelled over the noise from the engine and rotors. "Landslides and bad weather's already caused a major pile-up on the interstate to the northwest. They're stretched thin at Spruce Ridge General and when your call came through, all Medevac were engaged. You're lucky I was in the area."

"I'll go," Sam yelled, leaping into the helicopter with familiarity and an ease born of a well-conditioned body as he grabbed the collapsible gurney and pulled it inside. He slid it into place and hung the saline bag on an overhead hook before strapping the stretcher to the floor.

Cassidy felt her stomach clench into a tight ball of terror at the thought of flying through a blizzard. She'd heard stories about the late spring storms that often tore through the Cascades and wasn't looking forward to flying into it.

Swallowing her fear, she sucked in a lungful of cold air and shook her head decisively. Grasping the open door, she pulled herself inside before she could change her mind. "I'm the responsible physician at this hospital, Major," she yelled. "He's my patient. I can't let him go until I sign him over to another practicing physician." And when his dark gold gaze lifted and clashed with hers, she added a little more sharply, "My responsibility."

For a couple of beats Sam held her gaze then he gave a curt nod. "Fine. But I'm coming with you."

Ignoring the relief that slid into her stomach, Cassidy shook her head. "Not necessary. I...*we'll* be fine. I know you have other...plans."

He sent her a puzzled, narrow-eyed look that said he didn't know what she was talking about but wanted to demand an explanation. All he said was, "Be right back," before leaning forward to talk to the pilot, who was fiddling with the panel of overhead instruments. After a couple of beats the pilot nodded and Sam clasped the man's shoulder. Moving to the open door, he flashed an inscrutable look in her direction then jumped from the helo to lope across the helipad towards the building.

The rotors picked up speed and Cassidy swallowed hard. *Oh, God.* She hoped he hurried back before she changed her mind. Besides, she'd overheard a couple of nurses discussing meeting up with him later, which meant he was probably cancelling their date—or rescheduling.

And since he'd made it clear he wasn't in the market for anything long term and *she'd* made it clear she wouldn't get involved with a colleague, there wasn't much left to say.

Was there?

So why did she feel on the verge of tears? Why did she feel as though she'd just eaten a gallon of double-cream ice cream? Was she just having a panic attack at the idea of fly-

ing through a storm in a helicopter? Or was the queasy feeling in her stomach something else? But since she refused
to consider the "something else" and wasn't some damsel
in distress who needed to be rescued by a big, strong man,
she didn't know where that left her.

She checked Jim's vitals in an effort to calm her nerves,
tugged at the straps holding the gurney in place and fiddled
with his shoulder dressing. After an anxious look in the direction in which Sam had gone, she flicked at a few bubbles
in the IV line, hooked up another unit of blood, and then
*re*checked his vitals, aware that with every passing second
their window of opportunity for flying out was narrowing.

Finally, when her anxiety was at fever pitch, Sam reap-
peared. Without a word, he tossed her a thick parka, extra
blanket and rucksack before leaping into the chopper. He
pulled the door closed behind him, abruptly shutting out
the worst of the rotor roar and the first snowflakes.

Cassidy bit her lip and slid onto the bench seat, pressing a hand to her roiling belly as he leant forward to tap
the pilot on the shoulder. Without turning, the man lifted
his hand in acknowledgement and in the next instant the
engines screamed.

Cassidy dug her fingers into the bench seat beneath her.
The craft shuddered and she squeezed her eyes shut in an
effort not to freak out as the chopper lifted with a sickening
lurch and the ground abruptly disappeared beneath her feet.

Biting back a whimper, her grip on the bench tightened until her knuckles ached and her fingers turned white.
Something dropped around her shoulders an instant before
Sam's heat enveloped her. He pressed his solid shoulder
close as a big, calloused hand covered hers. Once he'd pried
her fingers loose, he engulfed them in a firm, warm clasp.

With his rough palm sliding against hers, he laced their
fingers together and gave her a comforting squeeze. Cassidy tightened her grip when what she really wanted to do
was climb into his lap and hide her face against his strong,

wide chest. She'd die of mortification later, she told herself, when her feet were once again firmly on solid ground.

His cold lips brushed her ear. "You can open your eyes now," he yelled, and she shook her head, unwilling to see the masculine amusement gleaming in his eyes.

God, she'd missed looking into those gold eyes...missed him *more than she'd thought possible.*

She felt his mouth smile against her temple and shivered as hot and cold goose bumps broke out across her skin. She was unsure if it was fear, the dipping temperatures or... or a desperate need for his touch—and terrified it was a combination of all three. For some reason his proximity always seemed to trigger a confusing mix of emotions that left her reeling.

"*Babe*," he said against her ear, and Cassidy could hear the smile in his voice before he gave her earlobe a gentle nip. This time she had no trouble identifying the origin of the shivers racing over her skin. "I won't let anything happen to you," he promised deeply. "I'm a SEAL. You're absolutely safe."

Cassidy turned to yell at him for calling her babe, only to find him less than an inch away. His gaze was hot, intense and a weird sensation of vertigo sent her stomach plummeting. For the second time in as many minutes her world tilted, and she was fairly certain it had nothing to do with being suspended above the earth in a flimsy aircraft.

Every thought fled save the sudden jumble of emotions she struggled to make sense of. Blood rushed from her head. Her lungs constricted and she was forced to acknowledge that she wasn't just hanging in space with a thin layer of metal between her and the jagged peaks below. Her heart was too—for an entirely different reason.

It quivered in her chest and before she could pull back from the edge or rip her hand from his and retreat to the opposite bench—*hell, throw herself from the helicopter*—

in an effort to protect herself, he lifted her hand to his lips and—*Oh, God*—pressed a kiss to her white knuckles.

A sob rose in her chest.

"I won't let anything happen to you," he repeated, with a reassuring smile that promised everything she'd told herself she didn't want and he couldn't possibly mean. And when she simply shook her head and squeezed her eyes shut, he cupped her jaw in his big, warm hand. He waited until her lashes rose before adding, "SEAL's honor."

Cassidy's heart clenched—his expression, and the heart-felt assurance, appearing more meaningful than a kiss. She sucked in a shuddery breath, suddenly terrified about what it could mean and blurted, "If we go down I'm going to kill you," as she battled with the shocking truth.

He laughed and her chest tightened painfully.

Oh, God.

She could no longer hide it from herself. She wasn't just fighting feelings for him. She was in love with Samuel J. Kellan, US Navy SEAL. A man who kept himself locked up tight, a man who didn't return her feelings, even though he wanted to be with her.

For now.

He'd wormed his way under her defenses and had settled next to her heart while making it perfectly clear she was a distraction. He didn't do long term and thinking she could matter to him was insane.

"Hey…" Sam's deep voice was laced with concern "…why the gloomy face?"

She dropped her lashes to hide her chaotic thoughts and bit her lip. Right, like she'd tell *him*. He already knew how to make her respond to him. She would rather die than have him guess how she felt.

Her pulse fluttered. He was such a beautiful man, strong, honorable and honest. He hadn't lied or made promises he knew he couldn't keep, and she couldn't imagine him tak-ing a woman hostage after he'd been caught doing something illegal and realized he could no longer sweet talk his way out of it. He wasn't Lance Turnbull. He'd proved time and again that he could be counted on. That he was someone worthy of love. That he was worthy of her love.

Only thing was: he didn't want it.

She gave a wild little laugh and hoped he thought she was freaking out about flying. "You ask that when we're a thousand feet over the Cascades—in a tin can?"

His eyes crinkled and his mouth curled into a quick grin that had her breath catching in her chest. For the first time since that night in the jail cell he looked relaxed and… carefree. *Happy,* even.

"Isn't it great?"

Yes, it was, she admitted silently, but not the view out the window. With a sudden flash of insight she realized that he missed his team, his dangerous job. And she wondered for perhaps the hundredth time why he chose to be stuck in a small mountain hospital, treating runny noses and hypertension, instead of jumping from aircraft, yelling "*Hoo-yah*" as he took out the enemy. And if, for just a fleeing moment, she wished she'd been responsible for the dazzling pleasure lighting his gold eyes, Cassidy reminded herself that kind of thinking would only lead to heartache. Heartache she knew—with abrupt certainty—she would never recover from.

She loved him but would keep her heart safely hidden. For now she would simply enjoy the warm, masculine scent of him and the press of his body against hers, knowing it would soon be gone.

"You're insane," she yelled, and rolled her eyes when his quick answering grin flashed with wicked recklessness. And when his eyes dropped to her mouth, her blood turned hot.

An odd expression crossed his face and his eyes darkened. "Yeah," he agreed, wrapping a hand around her head to tug her close. Expecting his usual fiery mastery, Cassidy was stunned when his mouth touched hers gently in a kiss that was as sweet as it was unexpected.

And before she could remember that this was a very bad idea, she was sliding her hands up to cup his hard, beard-roughened jaw. She opened for him, tentatively touching her tongue to his, while she fought the aching need squeezing her heart.

He tasted of hot, untamed man and for once in her life Cassidy wanted to leap off the edge, uncaring where she landed. There was only *this*—this wild, exciting moment with this wild, exciting man.

Tilting her head to give him room, she traced the strong line of his jaw with questing fingers, ignoring the tiny voice of reason in her head that warned she was heading for disaster. She didn't care. She just wanted to feel what was suddenly the most significant kiss of her life.

If this was all she'd have, she would take it. But she had to remind herself they weren't alone. With supreme effort, she broke off to say, "Sam, we should stop," hoping he would make it easy for her, and hoping with equal intensity that he would not.

With a savage growl Sam leaned his forehead against hers and sucked in a ragged breath. His heart thundered in his chest like he was having a coronary, yet he felt more alive than he had in a long time. More intensely aware of his surroundings—as though electricity flowed across his skin and connected every atom in his body to the universe. To her.

Pulling back an inch, he stared into misty green eyes heavy with arousal and emotions he couldn't begin to identify, and wondered briefly what had made this kiss so different.

He was thirty-four years old, and he'd just had the hottest, wildest kiss of his life in a cold, noisy helicopter a couple of thousand feet in the air—with a woman who wasn't interested in a relationship and then kissed like she was searching for his soul.

Reminding himself that his time in Crescent Lake was running out—that this was just a fantasy interlude before he returned to his real life—Sam caught her mouth in a brief, scorching kiss. "Later," he growled, sliding his gaze over her face as though committing the soft confusion in her eyes to memory.

Damn, but she was so beautiful.

Suddenly her eyes widened and she pulled away so abruptly he cast around for the threat before he realized she was dropping to her knees beside Jim.

"He's crashing," she yelled, pulling at the straps securing the stretcher. Cursing himself for forgetting where they were, Sam leaned over to release the safety clip as Cassidy tore off the blanket to expose the patient's chest. She checked his pulse and immediately began performing CPR as Sam grabbed a headset to bark at the pilot.

Learning they were less than five minutes out of Spruce Ridge, he instructed the pilot to radio ahead with their ETA and to have a resus team waiting at the helipad. He tossed aside the headset and dug into his rucksack for the supplies he'd thrown there earlier.

He ripped off the plastic needle cover with his teeth and plunged the syringe into the vial of atropine. With a smooth one-handed move that might have impressed Cassidy if her patient hadn't been in trouble, he drew back the plunger.

"Get that into his vein," she ordered sharply, before stopping the chest compressions to begin mouth-to-mouth. The following minutes were filled with the urgency only experienced by medics concerned with saving a life, and by the time they landed and rushed him across the helipad, Jim Bowen's pulse was once again steady.

The ortho specialist was already suiting up when Cassidy followed her patient into the OR. The gray-haired surgeon's piercing blue gaze studied her over the top of his spectacles as he thrust his hands into latex gloves.

"Grant Sawyer, orthopedic specialist," he introduced himself brusquely. "Mahoney from Crescent Lake?" And when she nodded, he barked, "Fill me in."

Cassidy gave a succinct report of their intervention while the theatre staff prepped Jim for surgery. Sawyer listened and nodded as he skimmed through the patient's chart.

"Good job," he said with a brusque nod, and turned away to rap out orders for blood and instruments, leaving Cassidy with the impression that she'd just been dismissed.

She backed out of the OR, fighting the feeling that she should be doing something. *Anything* but stand around while others worked miracles.

Sam was waiting in the hallway. "You okay?" he asked, shoving off the wall he'd been propping up. Cassidy nodded absently and pushed the tousled hair off her forehead. "Why?"

"Resus says ER's swamped and could use some help. You up for it?"

"We're not flying back?"

Sam shook his head. "Storm's too bad. We're lucky we made it before all aircraft were grounded. Pilot's already gone and all roads into the mountains have been closed."

Cassidy's belly clenched. "So we're…stuck."

Sam placed a warm hand into the small of her back and sent her a crooked grin. "Just you and me, babe. Until morning."

Cassidy rolled her eyes at his use of the hated word that was strangely enough starting to grow on her. "And an ER full of accident victims."

"Yeah." He laughed dryly, steering her down the wide hallway. "And that."

* * *

Hours later Cassidy pulled off her latex gloves and made the last notations on her clipboard. Darkness had long fallen and the storm had turned the world beyond the hospital walls white and icy. Fortunately the number of casualties had dwindled to a trickle and she could finally take a break.

She was also starving.

Stretching tired muscles, Cassidy wandered out to the waiting room and handed the clipboard to the woman manning the nurses' station. "Finally packing it in, honey?" the nurse asked with a sympathetic smile.

"You're good to go," Cassidy replied, smoothing her messy hair off her face and twisting it at the back of her head, where she pinned it using a couple of pins someone had found for her. "Have you seen Major Kellan?"

"Big handsome hunk with the pretty eyes?"

Cassidy smiled at the woman's description. "That's him."

"I saw him heading towards the doctors' lounge with the ER manager about ten minutes ago," the nurse reported and eyed Cassidy with open envy. "You two…together?"

"Yes," she said with a small smile, and turned to head down the passage. They were together but not *together*. She didn't think any woman could say she and Samuel Kellan were…*together*. He didn't do together with anyone—which should have made her feel better but didn't, especially when she entered the doctors' lounge and found him surrounded by admirers.

Almost immediately he turned, a warm, intimate smile curling his lips when their gazes met and held. He quickly excused himself and headed across the room to wrap his hands around her upper arms and yank her against him. Her squeak of surprise was abruptly cut off by his openmouthed kiss, and before she could react, he'd sucked out her brain along with her breath.

Several long seconds later Sam broke off the kiss and

lifted his head a couple of inches. "Hey," he murmured, his rough, deep voice sliding against her like a heated caress.

She gulped in a shocked breath and gaped at him. "Wh-what…?" Her mouth snapped shut on her stuttered attempt at coherence. Besides, they were standing in a brightly lit doctors' lounge filled with openly staring medical personnel.

"Work with me here, babe," he said out of the corner of his mouth. Baffled by his unexpected behavior, Cassidy opened her mouth again. "What…?" but Sam was tugging her into the hallway.

"*Hey*," she complained, and tugged against his grip. "Coffee. Now. Maybe even intravenously."

Sam grimaced. "Forget about that swill. I've got something better."

Her mouth dropped open and she stared at him in shocked silence before sliding her gaze down his hard belly to his crotch. *Did he…? Could he really…?*

"*Doc!*" Sam's eyes widened but he was also battling a grin. "You have a dirty mind," he accused, and when she just rolled her eyes he spun her around and hustled her back against the nearest wall, his body following.

Surprised by the slick move, Cassidy gave a startled squeak even as his mouth closed over hers, and then he was kissing her like he couldn't wait to get her naked. She slapped a hand against his chest and made a gurgling sound in her throat.

Sam reluctantly backed off, looking a little wild. Cassidy flushed and tried to shove him away but he leaned into her and rasped out, "Give me a minute." She opened her mouth to tell him he'd had his minute when she felt something large and hard poking her belly. She froze, her flush deepening, until she was sure she was glowing like a neon sign in the desert.

"What is it with you and walls?" she huffed out, secretly

grateful for the hard body keeping her upright. His gold eyes gleamed at her through thick dark eyelashes.

"If I don't take advantage of the nearest one," he growled, "you'd be practicing those sneaky evasion techniques you've perfected over the past few weeks."

Cassidy opened her mouth to reply when her stomach growled and she dropped her head back and closed her eyes in defeat. Sam chuckled and pushed away from the wall.

"Looks like you need more than coffee."

"I'm starving," she excused herself with a faint blush. "I wonder what the hospital cafeteria is serving."

Sam grimaced and stepped back, his hand sliding down to circle her wrist. "Nothing good, believe me." He gave her a gentle tug closer. "Let's go."

"Where? I'm starving."

His eyebrow rose at her petulant tone. "And I'm going to feed you," he promised. "Just not here. I managed to get us a room at a hotel a couple of blocks away."

Shock and panic moved through Cassidy. "*What?* No!"

Sam's brow rose. "No?"

"No," Cassidy said shortly. "I'm not sharing a room with you."

He sent her a chiding look. "Now, *babe*—" he began.

Only to have Cassidy interrupting with, "I beg your pardon?"

He grinned, leaving her head reeling at his abrupt mood changes. "You really shouldn't try that icy debutante tone with me, Doc."

"Excuse me?"

He leaned closer with a sinful grin that sent alarm and heat arrowing through her. "Makes me hot," he murmured against her ear, and Cassidy felt her cheeks heat. She could feel exactly how hot.

She edged away. "I can get my own room, Sam." No way could she spend the night with him and not expose herself.

Her feelings were too new, too raw—and she was terrified she would just blurt them out in the heat of the moment.

"No, Cassidy, you can't." And when she scowled he smoothed his hand down to the base of her spine and tugged her closer. "And not just because you didn't bring cash or cards. The hotels in the area are all full. I checked. I was lucky, *really* lucky to get that room."

His look was carefully casual. "So, dinner and the last room at the inn?"

Cassidy sighed and made a helpless gesture. "Sam—"

He captured her hand. "Look," he interrupted quietly, "I know you don't get involved with people you work with. But we're not colleagues here. We're just a man and a woman who are attracted to each other."

She looked up in surprise. "I thought—."

He shrugged out of his parka and wrapped it around her shoulders as he steered her towards the main entrance. "You thought what?"

Looking up into his handsome face, Cassidy recalled the conversation she'd overheard earlier that day. "I know you were planning to meet up with some of the nurses later."

His stopped abruptly. "What?"

She licked her lips and exhaled noisily, hoping he couldn't see how much the knowledge hurt. "I understand. Really. It's not like we're—" She stopped abruptly and looked away, unable to continue.

Sam folded his arms across his chest. "Not like we're what, Cassidy?"

She swallowed and smoothed her tousled hair off her face, looking anywhere but at him and feeling unaccountably flustered. "It's not like we're...well, together. Or anything," she ended lamely.

His mouth compressed into a hard line and a muscle jumped in his jaw. "Well, you apparently know more than I do," he growled. "*Jeez*. You don't have a very good opinion of men, do you? Or is it just me?"

Startled by his mercurial moods, Cassidy stared up at him. "What are you talking about?

His jaw clenched. "I'm talking about the fact that you think I'd have sex with other women just because you're avoiding me."

She flushed. Okay, so that's exactly what she'd thought. "Sam—"

"Cassidy," he mocked gently, and cradled her face between his warm palms. "It's just you," he murmured, his eyes a deep dark gold that had her heart lurching in silly feminine hope. Was he saying what she thought he was saying? "Since that night in county lock-up, it's been you."

For now, she wanted to add, but didn't want to ruin the fragile mood between them. Sucking in a shaky breath, she sent him a falsely bright smile and shored up the cracks in her composure. She'd take what she could and protect her heart later. When he was gone.

"I think you promised me dinner," she murmured, and his grin was quick and white in his dark face. Leaning forward, he planted a hard kiss on her mouth. "That's just the appetizer, *babe*," he promised quietly. "We have the whole night to savor the main course."

CHAPTER ELEVEN

CASSIDY WOKE ON a surge of adrenaline, abruptly and fully alert between one breath and the next. Heart pounding in her chest, she blinked into the darkness and struggled with a sense of disorientation.

Quickly taking stock, she realized she wasn't at home in Boston and she wasn't in her bed at the inn. But she *was* naked, which could only mean one thing...*Sam!*

Fear and a gut-deep knowledge that something was very wrong had her rolling over in the wide bed just as she heard it again—harsh, ragged. There was a heavy thud and something crashed to the floor, instantly followed by a litany of snarled curses.

Pulse spiking with alarm, she lurched upright and tried to recall where the bedside lamp was situated. His abruptly yelled, "*No! No!*" sent chills streaking up her spine, and a quick tactile reconnaissance of the mattress confirmed she was alone in the bed. Was Sam fighting some psycho who'd sneaked into their hotel room?

"He's just a kid, for God's sake. Let him go... *God*, let him go."

He? Who was he talking about? Heck, who was he talking to?

A low, threatening sound vibrated deep in his throat, making the hair on her body stand on end before a babble of foreign words filled the room, menacing and a little frightening.

Launching herself across the bed, she fumbled for the light switch, rapping her elbow on the bedside table and almost knocking the lamp over in her haste. She finally located the switch and blinked against the sudden light bursting into the room.

She didn't know what she'd expected but it wasn't Sam fighting an unseen enemy. *Oh, God,* she thought. Was he experiencing a flashback or having a nightmare?

A murderous bellow had Cassidy's heart rate spiking. She watched wide-eyed as he struggled violently, arms pinned to his side, tendons, sinew and well-defined muscles straining beneath acres of sweat-slicked skin.

He was gloriously naked, but for once she failed to appreciate the perfect lines of his hard body. Her gaze was locked on his face. His shadowed features contorted with fury as he lurched around the room, crashing into everything in his path. It was a wonder he didn't wake up with all the noise he was making and Cassidy wondered if he was reliving some actual or imagined event.

He suddenly stiffened, and with a hoarse, anguished "*No!*" he jolted like he'd been struck. Then he slowly sank to his knees, his breath coming in ragged dry heaves.

Biting back the cry that rose to her lips, Cassidy pressed herself against the headboard, wanting desperately to go to him. She *needed* to go to him—especially when he thrust his hands through his hair and she got her first good look at his face. He looked completely and utterly devastated.

No longer able to keep her distance, she slid from the bed and approached him warily, desperate to comfort him. A hoarse moan tore from his throat and the desolation in the sound lifted the hair at the nape of her neck. She halted a few feet away and dropped to her knees, the sight of his wet cheeks wrenching at her tender heart. Unbearable pressure squeezed her chest in a giant fist and before she could stop it from happening, her newly exposed heart quivered…and broke.

A sob rose in her throat and she reached out a hand, her trembling fingers sliding greedily over the rounded ball of his shoulder. His skin, normally so warm, was damp and cold to the touch and her medical training took over. She wasn't a psychiatrist, but working in ER she'd witnessed enough cases of psychological trauma to know shock when she saw it.

"Samuel," she said firmly, rubbing his wide shoulder in slow, soothing movements. For long moments he remained unresponsive, the room filled with nothing but his harsh breathing—his body shaking as shudders moved through him. "Sam. Wake up, you're dreaming."

His muscles turned to stone beneath her hand as he abruptly stilled. He slowly lifted his head, turning a gaze completely stripped of emotion in her direction. He looked at her as though he didn't know her and wasn't quite sure what she was doing there.

Tension radiated off him like a nuclear blast and she braced herself for his reaction. But after long tense moments he blinked as though coming out of a trance, confusion pulling at his dark brows.

"Cassidy?" His voice emerged, hoarse and a little rusty. Her shoulders sagged and her breath escaped in a relieved whoosh that left her trembling and dizzy.

Okay, she thought, *so far so good.*

Shifting closer, she carefully smoothed a line from his shoulder to his bulging biceps and curled her fingers into his inner arm where the satin-smooth flesh was clammy. A fine tremor twitched the muscles beneath her hand. Even in the dim light his pallor was evident, as was the fine sheen of perspiration, the dazed disorientation in his eyes. She pushed damp hair off his forehead with her free hand before cupping his hard, beard-roughened jaw in her palm.

Staring into his distressed eyes, she whispered, "It's

okay, Sam…I'm here," fighting the need to wrap her arms around him, to press her body close, share her warmth. Protect him from his demons. "I'm here."

After a couple of beats he lifted unsteady fingers to brush a light caress over her mouth. His tender touch, so at odds with the violence she'd sensed in him just moments ago, tore at her control, and a tear finally escaped, the accompanying sob a hot ball of razor-sharp emotions in her throat.

His eyes tracked the silvery tear before he caught it near her mouth with the tip of one long tanned finger.

"You're crying." He sounded baffled, concerned, as another tear escaped, then another.

Horrified by her slipping control, she covered his hand with hers and turned her face into his wide, calloused palm, choking back emotions that seemed to be rising faster than Biblical flood waters.

Get a grip, Mahoney. The guy needs your strength here, not tears and certainly not any declarations of love.

"I… It's nothing," she replied softly, nuzzling his hand, her gaze clinging to his as though he would vanish if she blinked. "Something happened. Tell me about it."

If Cassidy had blinked she might have missed the shield slamming down between them. Between one breath and the next his eyes cleared as he abruptly withdrew. All without moving a muscle. Then his hand slid out from beneath hers and he moved away, leaving her cold and oddly hollow.

The barrier was as tangible as a brick wall. Feeling suddenly exposed she hurriedly looked around for something to cover her nakedness. Spying his soft, well-washed T-shirt, she grabbed it and hastily pulled it over her head, surrounding herself with his familiar scent.

He was slumped back against the bed, wrists draped over his upraised knees, head bowed, breathing heavily as though he'd run ten miles in full gear up a steep mountain slope. His face was gray and emotional strain carved deep furrows beside the tense lines of his mouth.

Wishing she could comfort him and knowing it was the last thing he wanted from her, Cassidy felt raw emotion rise like a tide from her chest into her throat. She swallowed past the lump in her throat and wrapped her arms around herself to ward off the room's sudden chill.

"What happened?" she prompted softly.

A muscle ticked in his jaw and his face settled into a blank mask that squeezed her already bruised heart. For long moments he stared silently at the floor then exhaled noisily, thrusting a hand through his hair, the jerky motion dislodging a dark lock. She had to curl her fingers into her palm to keep from reaching out to smooth it away. Smooth his pain away.

After a moment he said flatly, "The mission was jinxed from the start. It was supposed to be quick. Drop in, find the hostages, blow everything up, go home. Instead there was a welcoming committee waiting at the drop site, as though they knew exactly where we were going to be." He pressed the heels of his hands against his eyes, looking unbearably weary.

"We barely had time to dive for cover before firepower erupted around us. Back-up was still miles away and we were pinned down from all sides. I remember thinking we'd bide our time, wait them out." He broke off with a bitter laugh. "Yeah, right. We'd expected maybe a dozen armed men. What we didn't figure was that our intel was compromised. There were maybe fifty heavily armed men. All with us in their sights."

He paused, face hard, hands curled into fists, as though he was reliving that night. After a few moments of silence he added, "Back-up was also taking heavy fire and before I knew it we were out of ammo and outmuscled. Finally they rounded us up and took us into the mountains, where we were questioned. Separately. Together—hoping we'd talk."

Cassidy had a feeling "questioned" meant tortured. She went cold at the thought and pressed a fist against her mouth to prevent a sound of distress from escaping.

"Did you?"

Sam's harsh laugh scraped at her ragged nerve endings. "Honey, SEALs don't talk. Ever." He took a couple of deep breaths before continuing. "They cut us off, took out our ground support and left us with no way to contact base command. We were on our own." He fell silent. "Then one night, about a week into our capture, they came for me," he said hollowly. "I remember thinking, *This is it, time to make peace with God.*" His eyes narrowed on some point in the past and he absently rubbed his wrists.

"What h-happened next?" Cassidy prompted softly, dreading what she sensed was coming.

He gave a heavy sigh. "They must have found out I was a medic," he said flatly, dropping his gaze between his large bare feet. "I was taken to a house in the village and told to treat some sick kid. I refused unless they let my team go." He snorted. "I had to try. Turned out they were waiting for a camera crew. An entire SEAL team is good leverage when you want scumbag terrorists released." He scrubbed his hands over his face. "I eliminated two guys before they…uh…subdued me."

Sick with horror, Cassidy tightened her grip on her arms. He didn't need to tell her what "eliminated" meant. She knew. Just as she knew "subdued" meant they'd probably beaten him senseless.

"Seemed they didn't want me dead. At least, not yet. Dead meant I couldn't save the kid, who was in pretty bad shape. I don't know how long I was out but by the time they emptied a bucket of water over me, they'd dragged in the team rookie and were holding a gun to his head. My eyes were practically swollen shut and my vision was blurring badly, but one look at him and I knew we were in trouble."

He muttered a few curses and wiped his face as though

he could wipe away the memories. "*Jeez*, they'd beaten Scooter until his mother wouldn't recognize him. But at least he was still alive. Anyway, I said I'd treat the boy if they let me patch Scooter up. They argued amongst themselves for a while before finally agreeing." He laughed bitterly. "I knew…God, *knew*…I shouldn't trust them. I knew it, but I—"

He broke off abruptly, shifting restlessly, leaving Cassidy dreading the rest of the story. She could guess what was coming and braced herself, knowing that despite his training he'd been helpless to save the life of his friend.

"I asked for my med supplies and removed the kid's appendix. Took a couple of hours for his fever to break but when he finally opened his eyes, the guy with the gun on Scooter just looked me in the eye and…pulled the trigger." He sucked in a ragged breath and then for the first time since he'd begun he turned to look at her—eyes bloodshot, devastated as he relived the nightmare.

"They shot him," he said blankly, as though he still couldn't believe it. "They laughed and shot him in the head like a rabid stray." Shoving his fingers through his hair, he looked away and struggled for control as Cassidy battled against the urge to hold him close, promise things he didn't want or need from her.

After a few moments he sucked in a ragged breath and added, "I went berserk. I took out everyone and secured the kid's mother before she could rouse the whole damn village. Then I went to get my team."

"Oh, Sam," she rasped, heartsick at how unbearably sad he looked, how unendurably weary. And she could no longer ignore the compulsion to touch him. But when she reached for him he abruptly turned away, as though he couldn't bear her touch. She bit her lip against the devastating hurt of his rejection and slowly lowered her hand.

"I'd do it again," he vowed softly, his tone deadly. "They tortured and killed half my team. Good men…my brothers, my friends…and I….they were my responsibility and I failed them. If I'd made my move sooner, Scooter would still be alive."

"Or maybe not," Cassidy offered softly. "Maybe you'd both be dead."

He rounded on her with a furious snarl, a white blaze of hot fury in his eyes. "It would have been nothing more than I deserved," he snarled, rising abruptly. "I'm a SEAL. Failure is *not* an option."

He looked around a little wildly, as though he'd found himself trapped. Movements jerky with suppressed violence, he snatched up jeans, socks and boots and dressed in simmering silence. He'd shoved his arms through the sleeves of his flannel shirt and grabbed his jacket before she realized he was leaving.

"Samuel, wait." She reached out to tangle shaking fingers in soft flannel before she realized she'd moved. He stilled but didn't turn, his stiff posture broadcasting louder than words that he was barely hanging on to his control.

"Where are you going?"

"Out."

Feeling him slipping away, she did the one thing she'd promised herself she would never do. She begged.

"*Please*, Sam, don't go. Stay. Talk to me."

Ignoring her plea, he silently reached for the door, and before she knew she was moving, Cassidy slipped around his body to press her back against the door. He looked momentarily surprised, even retreated a step before his features hardened and his laser-bright gaze sliced her to ribbons.

Ignoring the aggression pumping off him in waves, Cassidy locked her wobbling knees and bravely held his gaze, aware that she was shaking inside. She had a feeling if she let him go she'd never see him again.

For a long tension-filled moment he stared at her, eyes blazing with emotions so raw and violent that she had to force her body not to step into his. "Stay, Sam…just *stay*," she pleaded hoarsely.

A muscle flexed in his jaw and she realized with shock that he was shaking too. She wanted to go to him but was held in place by the invisible *keep out* signs radiating off him. Finally he gritted through clenched teeth, "There is nothing to say. Now move out the way, Doc. I don't want to hurt you."

Doc? He was calling her Doc after everything they'd shared?

Swallowing a bitter laugh, Cassidy drew in a shuddery breath and tried not to show how much his words—heck, his attitude—hurt. "I…love you Sam," she whispered hoarsely.

His gaze sharpened as though he'd heard her but intended to ignore her ragged confession. "It's just a walk, Cassidy," he said roughly. "I need some air." And when she held out her hand, his coldly furious "I don't need a goddamn nursemaid, for God's sake. I just want some damn air. Is that too much to expect?" had her jaw dropping open in shock.

Recovering quickly, she stepped forward to flatten her palm against his naked chest, hoping her touch would somehow get through the impenetrable wall he'd built around himself. "I… Let me help you, Samuel," she blurted out before she could stop herself. "Please, don't go. I…I love you. I love you, let me help."

His reaction was swift and shockingly direct. Jerking back as if she'd slapped him, he stared at her in silence for a couple stunned beats before his expression turned into a remote mask, rejection clear in every tense line of his body.

Cassidy's heart sank and she pressed a shaking hand against the hard cold ball of misery forming in her throat. "Sam—?"

"I'm sorry," he interrupted impassively, frowning at her as though he'd never seen her before, and the cold ball of dread dropped into her chest, lodging right where her heart should be.

Two words, *I'm sorry*, were suddenly the most devastating of her life. More devastating than anything that had happened in Boston. "You're...s-s-sorry?"

He gave a heavy sigh. "Yes." His handsome face was carved with cold disinterest, his once beautifully glowing eyes flat and detached—as though she were a stranger. A stranger he didn't particularly like the look of. "I'm flattered, of course, but I thought you understood I wasn't..." He made a sound of annoyance. "Well, I'm sorry you believed otherwise. Now please step aside, I don't want to hurt you."

Cassidy didn't remember moving, could only watch as he opened the door and walked out without a backward glance. Hours later, when a firm knock sounded at the door, she flew across the room, wild hope and relief shriveling along with her heart when she opened to find not Samuel but the Forestry Services pilot.

Once the pilot left, Cassidy moved around the room like an automaton, gathering her clothing and dressing in stunned silence. She carefully washed and dried her face, ignoring the white-faced stranger in the mirror as she pulled her hair off her face and secured it at the nape of her neck. Then with her raw, bleeding heart carefully locked away behind a coolly professional façade, she left the hotel and headed for the hospital to check on Jim before taking the elevator to the helipad.

She scarcely remembered the flight back to Crescent Lake. Staring sightlessly out the window, she was impervious to the cold, the stunning scenery, the curious man at her side.

Nothing. She felt absolutely...*nothing*.

By the time the chopper touched down, Cassidy was grateful for the numbness. She even managed to aim a small smile of thanks at the pilot before alighting from the helicopter. The ground was slippery with ice as she carefully picked her way to the building.

Fran Gilbert took one look at Cassidy's face and the blood drained away from her face, leaving her pale and concerned. "What's wrong?" she demanded. "Are you okay? Is Jim okay?"

Drawing her professionalism around her like a cloak, Cassidy paused to reassure the older woman. "He's holding steady," she said. "I checked on him before I left and spoke to his doctor. He seems cautiously optimistic about Jim's recovery."

"I'll call his wife," Fran said with relief but kept her gaze sharply on Cassidy's face then voiced the question Cassidy had been dreading. "Where's Samuel?"

Cassidy wrapped her arms around herself and forced herself not to react. "I… He had to leave suddenly."

Fran looked surprised, confused. "Leave? Where did he go?"

Cassidy shrugged as though her heart wasn't a bloodied, pulpy mess. "I don't know," she admitted, pressing trembling fingers against her aching temple. "His message didn't say."

Fran digested the news in silence before saying, "You look awful, honey, and you're frozen to the bone. Are you sick?"

Cassidy didn't believe her attempt to smile fooled the other woman but she was beyond caring. She was barely holding onto her composure as it was and Fran had just given her the perfect excuse. "I think I've caught a bug," she croaked, instantly ashamed when Fran looked concerned.

"Oh, honey, do you need someone to drive you home?" Fran asked, gently rubbing some warmth into Cassidy's frozen arms. But she had a feeling nothing would ever make her feel warm again.

She shook her head and resisted the urge to drop her head onto Fran's shoulder. If she did, she would shatter into a million pieces and she couldn't do that until she was alone.

"I can't leave, Fran," she croaked, her control slipping fast. "Now that…um…" She swallowed hard and drew in a shaky breath. "Now that the major is gone, I'll need to pull double shifts." Besides, being busy would keep her from thinking too much.

"No, you won't," Fran reproached firmly. "You'll go home and get into bed. We'll handle things today." And when Cassidy opened her mouth to argue she said, "No arguments. I promise to call if we have an emergency."

Cassidy stared into Fran's gentle blue eyes and finally pulled away. The woman knew. *Oh, God, was she that obvious?*

"I'll get my purse and jacket."

Cassidy let herself into the inn, aware that she was shaking uncontrollably as if she'd contracted some kind of jungle fever. Sweat slicked her skin and she had to wipe her damp palm against her thigh several times before she could shove the key into the lock.

Sudden dizziness swamped her one instant, the next her stomach cramped violently and the hand that she'd flung out to grab the doorframe slapped over her mouth instead. She made a mad dash for the bathroom at the end of the hall, barely slamming the door behind her before she lost the meager contents of her stomach.

When the retching finally stopped, she dragged herself to her feet. Moving to the basin to rinse her mouth, she caught sight of herself in the mirror and couldn't hold back a horrified gasp. She was paper-white, hollow-eyed and looked like she'd just survived a major disaster. No wonder Fran was concerned, she thought, eyeing herself dispassionately. She looked like hell. And felt much worse.

Unfortunately, the numbness that had got her through the past six hours was fading and the awful truth of what had happened was finding its way through the cracks in her composure.

Her eyes and her throat burned with unshed tears and her heart felt like he'd ripped open her chest and savaged her. Hurrying back to her room before the dam burst, Cassidy shoved the door closed and she was finally—*finally*—alone.

She sank back against the door, her knees buckling as a ragged sob escaped and the first scalding tear eased over her lashes to carve a fiery path down her cheek. By the time her bottom hit the floor, keening sobs racked her body and the tight leash she'd kept on her emotions finally snapped.

It was over, she told herself. *Over.* When she'd finally admitted to feelings she'd never intended to feel.

Dropping her forehead onto her updrawn knees, she choked back a ragged cry. Samuel J. Kellan had rocked her world then walked away without a backward glance. As if she meant less than nothing.

He'd made mad, passionate love to her then coldly, dispassionately, told her he was sorry she loved him. He was flattered—*flattered*—but thought she'd understood he wasn't looking for a relationship. *I'm sorry you believed otherwise,* he'd said, slicing her to the soul. And then, when she'd stared at him, her shattered heart exposed for the world to see—for *him* to see—he'd calmly told her to step aside because he didn't want to hurt her.

He'd calmly crushed her heart…and left.

CHAPTER TWELVE

CASSIDY ENTERED BERNIE'S supermarket and exchanged a few hurried greetings of "Hello, how are you feeling today?" and "Don't forget to bring the baby in for his next check-up." As much as she enjoyed stopping to chat, she hoped she could get in and out as quickly as possible.

She had a long list of items to get for a bachelorette party, in…she quickly glanced at her watch…*yikes,* less than two hours. She also had to get back to the inn and shower and change out of her jeans and stained scrubs top.

She was heading down the snack aisle, tossing things in her trolley, when she caught sight of the sheriff's car drive past and pull in across the street. Turning away with an irritated mutter, Cassidy checked the next item off her list.

She'd thought she was getting over being dumped in a Spruce Ridge hotel but then she'd heard Ruben Kellan's voice down the passage in ER. Her heart had sped up and stopped at the same time, which was not only impossible but alarming.

Her knees had turned to jelly and the blood had drained from her head so fast that Mrs. Jenkins—whom she'd been examining at the time—had shoved her into a chair and called for a nurse.

Cassidy had blamed the episode on lack of food and long hours. No one had said anything but she didn't think they believed her. Later Fran Gilbert had pulled her aside and handed her a pregnancy test. Cassidy remembered gaping at the other woman and dismissing the idea since Sam had used protection, but when she'd had a chance to think clearly, she realized she couldn't remember her last period.

So she'd panicked.

But when the results had shown up negative she'd cried, great big gulping sobs that hadn't made a bit of sense. She didn't *want* to be pregnant—at least, not like that—by a man who'd made mad, passionate love to her one minute, as though he couldn't get enough, then the next had walked out like she was nothing.

Except it had proved to be a turning point of sorts. She'd emerged from the bathroom bound and determined to get over him. She'd thrown herself into the community, introduced a monthly clinic day for the local schools and a mothers' support group that she hoped they'd continue after she was gone.

During her visit to the middle school she'd met art teacher Genna Walsch, and they'd become close friends. It was Genna's bachelorette party Cassidy was on her way to.

Whipping through the store, she piled items into her trolley before heading for the refrigeration section. She selected a few bottles of chilled champagne and then added fruit juice for pregnant guests.

Next she headed towards the deli, where she'd arranged to pick up a few roast chickens, and had to squeeze past two women studying the selection of cold cuts and chatting.

"I heard Patty Sue from the sheriff's office tell everyone he's coming back," the thirty-something blonde told her friend. "No one knows for sure if it's for good but rumor says it is. I've been surfing the net for obscure symptoms that will get me some quality time with him." She shivered dramatically. "I heard he's *real* good with his hands and I can't wait to play doc—"

The second woman caught sight of Cassidy and nudged her friend into silence, making her wonder what they'd been discussing. Or rather *whom* they'd been discussing. Just then the server turned with a welcoming smile and a "What can we do for you, Dr. Mahoney?" and Cassidy pushed the conversation from her mind.

She knew the county had hired two new doctors that were expected to start at the end of the month. She also knew she would have to make a decision about where to go once *her* contract expired.

As much as she told herself she was over Sam, Cassidy was honest enough to admit that living in the same town as his family meant it was fairly reasonable to expect him to visit occasionally. The longer she stayed in town, the greater the possibility of seeing him, and quite frankly she wasn't sure how she'd feel, or react, if she saw him again.

She'd made several enquiries and had received a couple of good offers—one of which was Spruce Ridge General—but she couldn't make up her mind. Frankly, she didn't want to leave. For the first time in her life she felt part of a community, like she was making a difference in people's lives. She liked feeling needed and appreciated, and she really liked seeing their health improve under her care. It was so much more satisfying than treating nameless masses day in and day out.

She thanked the server and turned, checking chicken off her list. And walked into a wall. Of muscle.

Opening her mouth on an automatic apology, she was instantly assailed by a masculine scent that was all too familiar. Barely an inch from her nose was a wide, hard chest covered in soft black cotton. She knew without looking up past the long tanned throat, strong jaw and poet's mouth to sleepy golden eyes, that she was inches away from the one person who was able to scramble her brain.

Samuel J. Kellan.

Her stomach clenched into a hot ball of dread and joy, and her heart squeezed in her chest. Taking a hasty step in retreat, she tightened her grip on the strap of her shoulder bag. The dimly lit aisle, the illuminated display cases behind her, the couple discussing what to have for dinner, *everything*...faded.

It was as if the universe had suddenly narrowed to just the two of them. Her skin hummed, her ears buzzed and it was only when her vision grayed at the edges that she realized she was holding her breath.

Expelling it on a shaky whoosh, Cassidy's gaze hungrily traced his handsome features. He'd lost weight and he looked tired. There was a healing laceration on his jaw and a bruise darkened his sharply defined cheekbone and the skin around one eye.

Despite his features being in shadow, he appeared tanned and amazingly fit. He looked...wonderful, even if the gaze he'd locked on her face was hooded and unreadable.

Her stomach clenched and her chest felt like a giant fist was squeezing the breath from her lungs. So many times over the past weeks she'd imagined seeing him again. Had even practiced what she would say. But nothing, *nothing* could have prepared her for the stark reality of being this close to him again after she'd convinced herself that she was over him.

Her spirits sank. She'd clearly miscalculated. And with the knowledge came a swift rise of self-directed anger. Okay, she was angry with him too. The jerk had made mad, passionate love to her and when she'd told him she loved him and *begged* him not to go, he'd ripped her heart out and told her he was sorry. Yes, well, she was sorry too—sorry she'd been stupid enough to fall for him.

Yet despite all that, she was glad to see him. Relieved he was alive and in one piece.

He was the first to break the awkward silence.

"Cassidy." The sound of his voice, as deep and rough as she remembered, brushed against jagged emotions and tugged at something deep and raw within her.

She swallowed what felt like ground glass in her throat. "Major," she said, inordinately pleased when her voice emerged coolly polite, as though they were nothing more than casual acquaintances.

His eyes narrowed and his face tightened before his features assumed an impassive mask. He widened his stance and folded his arms across his chest in a move that emphasized his wide shoulders and the bulge of his biceps straining the sleeves of his T-shirt. He was carelessly masculine in a way that made her heart speed up and her knees wobble. And it was suddenly all too painfully obvious that she wasn't going to get over him.

Ever.

She gulped. She'd been fooling herself. He was *it* for her. And nothing she did would stop this soul-deep yearning for him, this ache of knowing they weren't meant to be. That *she* wasn't meant to be—at least not for him.

And didn't that just...*suck*.

The urge to leave was suddenly overwhelming but his big, tough body blocked her way and the potent cocktail of pheromones and testosterone he exuded made her feel lightheaded. Oh, wait, that might be caused by food-shopping on an empty stomach. A stomach that was suddenly queasy.

Biting her lip to keep from falling apart, she turned and had to abruptly alter her course to evade the hand he lifted. Thinking he meant to touch her, she stumbled backwards and froze. She sucked in a startled breath and her gaze flew from the hand suspended in the air between them to his face. Something flashed in his gold eyes—something that looked like pain. But he recovered quickly, a shutter slamming down over his features, and she thought maybe she'd been mistaken. His arm dropped to his side.

"How have you been?" he asked softly, and Cassidy's eyes widened. She clenched her jaw to keep it from bouncing off the floor.

He was asking how she'd been? *Really?* After he'd emotionally savaged her in a hotel room then disappeared for five weeks without a word?

She stared at him for a long moment, tempted to just walk away, but a closer inspection of his features revealed lines of exhaustion and uncertainty. Uncertainty?

Yeah, right, she thought with a silent snort, and folded her arms beneath her breasts. "Um...great," she rasped, before clearing her throat and saying with a little more composure, "I'm fine. You?"

His forehead wrinkled as though her behavior baffled him and Cassidy couldn't prevent a little spurt of satisfaction. He was baffled by her behavior? *Well, tough*, she thought, straightening her spine as though the sight of him didn't make her want to simultaneously punch him and throw herself in his arms. Besides, he'd given up the right to be baffled by anything she did.

"Um...yeah, fine," he said absently, his eyebrows pulling his face into a scowl.

Ignoring the urge to trace the arrogant arch of his brows with her fingers, she nodded. "That's...good," she said vaguely. "Your...um, family must be relieved you're home safely." And after an awkward pause during which his intense stare sent flutters dropping into her stomach, she added lamely, "Well, excuse me."

She stepped around him and escaped towards the checkout counter. This time he didn't try to stop her. Instead, he followed, looking big and bad and deliciously dangerous.

He waited while she paid for her purchases, chatting with the checkout clerk. And before she could object, he hefted her packets, announced, "I'll walk you to your car," and headed for the exit. As though expecting her to follow.

She did, quickly, trying to head him off. "That's not necessary," she told him, and grabbed for the carry-bag handle. They engaged in a brief tug of war until Sam gently removed her hand and repeated quietly, "I'll walk you to your car," his gaze as implacable as his words. His mouth tightened when she seemed about to argue, then he stepped around her, turning to wait patiently for directions.

She stood indecisively for a few moments, wondering if she should just leave her groceries and bolt. But that would only prove he still had the power to affect her.

Shoving an errant curl off her face, Cassidy sighed impatiently. "This really isn't necessary, Major," she said huffily. "I can manage a few grocery bags and I'm sure you're busy. So…I won't detain you."

He studied her silently for a few moments before transferring all the bags to one hand. The other he wrapped around her arm and steered her out into the early evening.

Hunching her shoulders against the cool mountain air and the curious looks they were receiving, Cassidy sighed and stepped through the doors. The last thing she needed was him walking her to her car. She was hanging onto her control by her fingernails as it was.

"Where's your car?"

She shifted nervously and adjusted her shoulder bag. "Major—"

"We need to talk," he said quietly, implacably, and Cassidy welcomed the surge of anger that followed his announcement. *What the hell?*

Suddenly furious with him, and with herself, she swung to face him. "There's nothing to say, Major," she said tightly, coolly. "*Nothing.* In fact, you were more than clear about your feelings the last time we…spoke. I get it. I'm not stupid, recent behavior to the contrary. I can read between the lines. Now, if you'll give me my damn bags, I'll be on my way." She grabbed her bags and yanked. This time he allowed her to take one. The others he held out of reach. Growling, Cassidy spun away and headed purposefully for the stairs leading to the parking lot. He snagged her arm in a tight grip.

"Cassidy…"

And suddenly she'd had enough. More than enough,

actually. "*Don't!*" she snapped, ripping her arm from his grasp and turning away abruptly. She sucked in a ragged breath. "Just...*don't.*" Furious tears pricked the backs of her eyes and she swallowed past the lump of emotion threatening to choke her. She needed to escape before her rigid control snapped. "I...I have to go. G-goodbye, Major."

Sam followed silently and watched as she fumbled in her purse for the car keys. Locating them, she pressed the remote and even in the gathering dusk he saw her fingers tremble.

Feeling his gut clench, he reached out and closed his hand over hers. She jolted as though he'd prodded her with a shock stick. Her skin was cold to the touch and his grip tightened when she tried to yank away.

Dammit, I screwed up and now she can't even stand my touch, he thought, when that was all he wanted. He wanted to press up against her curvy body and bury his face into the soft, sweet hollow beneath her ear. He wanted to lick her smooth skin and breathe in her special fragrance— warm, slightly fruity and smelling of clean mountain air. A scent he'd craved with every breath he'd inhaled every second of every day he'd been away.

She hurriedly stepped away and waited tensely while he unlocked her car and stowed her bags on the backseat. He then opened the driver's door and held out her keys. She reached for them, careful not to touch him, and would have slid into the car if Sam hadn't abruptly pushed her back against the cool metal, knowing he couldn't let her go like this. Not after the past weeks. Weeks of hell when he'd missed her like an absent body part.

At first he hadn't understood what the hell was wrong with him. Even his commander had ripped him a new one after he'd blown off the psych eval.

He was supposed to be an invincible SEAL but he'd fallen apart—shared his nightmares and his guilt with her, for God's sake. He hated her knowing he was a cold-blooded killer. Okay, he'd killed to save himself and the rest of his team—but he'd killed in a cold rage. And he hadn't been able to bear the compassion, the sympathy in her eyes. He didn't deserve any of it. He didn't deserve her.

He didn't remember much about that night in Spruce Ridge, but he did remember what he'd said to her. And he felt ashamed.

Everyone thought he was still PTSD but Sam knew that wasn't why he'd been a basket case after that night.

Okay, he was still PTSD but that wasn't the problem, and it had taken him a couple of long weeks to realize exactly what *was*. He was missing something more important than his sanity. His heart. And *she* was his heart.

But all he could think about now was the feel of her soft curves against him. *God*, he'd missed this. Missed having her curvy body pressed against his—like he was finally home.

She made a sound of distress and tried to push him away, but Sam manacled her wrists and pressed them against the cool metal beside her head. Then he took advantage of her shocked gasp and swooped down to crush her mouth with his.

God, he thought, thrusting his tongue deep, hiding out in a desert cave, he'd thought of nothing but the feel of her in his arms, the taste of her in his mouth.

Her heart pounded as hard as his and she struggled to free herself but he wasn't letting go. Not now that he was finally where he belonged. For long moments she remained stiff in his arms, and then with a long throaty moan her body melted against him.

Heart pounding, he released her hands and abruptly broke the kiss, pressing his erection against her. *God*, he wanted—no, *needed*—her more than he'd wanted anything.

Resting his forehead against the roof of her car, he

gulped in air and prayed for control, but then she whispered his name, "Samuel," and the sound of it on her lips blew him away.

He thrust his hands onto the wild silvery mass framing her face and the next instant he was devouring her with a hot, hungry desperation he'd never realized he was capable of. It burned him up, a raging wildfire that swept away every thought, every need in a wave of hot primal craving.

His emotions, unrestrained and frantic, burned hot and fierce. His hands streaked over her in a desperate attempt to feel all of her—her soft silky heat, her firm, smooth flesh—and it was a moment before he realized her hands weren't trying to pull him close but push him away.

"Stop," she cried hoarsely. "*Samuel! Stop!*"

Shocked, he froze, his chest heaving with the effort of drawing air into his lungs.

"Stop?" he croaked, not believing he was hearing right. *"Stop?"*

A ragged sound of misery escaped her throat and she flattened her palms against his chest and shoved. Sam was so surprised that he staggered back a couple steps until his back hit the neighboring car.

"Wha—?"

"Leave me alone, Sam," she croaked, and with one desperate look she dived into her car, slammed the door and shoved the key into the ignition before he could move.

The engine engaged in a roar and the car shot out of the parking lot, barely missing a battered Ford truck and a shiny new SUV parked beneath the streetlight.

The last image he had was of her white face streaked with tears, and the knowledge that he'd caused them made his gut clench in sick shock. He'd made her cry. *Again.*

Sam watched as her taillights disappeared, feeling at once numb and devastated. Gutted, like he hadn't felt since he'd let his team down. And just like that night, his rage turned outward. A red tide of primal fury he knew he couldn't let loose on the good people of Crescent Lake.

Shoving his hand into his pocket, he palmed his keys and headed towards his SUV. He might not want to let his rage loose on his friends, but he knew exactly where he *could*.

The sheriff hit the doors of the Crash Landing with the heel of his hand and strode into the bar, expecting to call in for a dozen body bags.

After a crappy week, he'd gone home armed with a six-pack and a giant pizza topped with the works, hoping to relax in front of his big-screen TV. Seattle was playing San Francisco. It was just his luck the call from Dispatch came through as Seattle slammed the first puck into the opposition's net.

Expecting to wade into World War Three, Ruben halted three feet into the bar and blinked in the dim light, aware that his jaw had dropped open. About a dozen men were propped up against the bar, tossing back tequila like they were practicing for a Mexican showdown and singing off-key enough to make tone-deaf ears bleed.

Pushing his hat up his forehead, Ruben shoved his hands on his hips and gaped at the spectacle. Sam was in the thick of things, arm slung around Chris Hastings as though they were bosom buddies when Ruben knew damn well and good they'd been enemies in high school. He'd never seen a sorrier bunch of idiots.

He strode up to the bar and pushed his way through the throng. The owner, watching the proceedings from behind the counter with an unreadable expression, nodded when he saw Ruben.

"Sheriff," he said. "Can I get you something?"

"Coffee, Joe. Strong, black with plenty of sugar."

Joe Montana lifted a brow and grinned. "One cup or two?"

"Make that two. And don't skimp on the sugar."

By the time Joe slid two coffees across the counter the men at the bar had left or wandered away, leaving the brothers alone.

"Go away," Sam growled, and defiantly lifted the last shot to his mouth. Ruben hastily removed the glass and shoved the coffee at him.

"Drink," he said shortly. "And then tell me what Crescent Lake's newest doctor is doing practicing for *America's Got No Talent*."

Sam grimaced at the cup in front of him. "Real funny."

"Not when I've been called away from a game where Seattle scored the first point against 'Frisco. Not when my *brother* is propping up Joe's bar and making people's ears bleed." Sam opened his mouth to argue but Ruben beat him to it. "Drink the damn coffee before I slap your ass in jail for disturbing the peace."

Sam scowled at him through bleary eyes for a couple of beats before he gave a heavy sigh and complied. "I was ready to quit anyway."

Ruben waited until Sam had consumed half the cup's contents before he said mildly, "Care to tell me what's going on?"

Sam shoved a hand through his hair and stared down into his half-empty cup. "Nothing." *Everything.* He'd glimpsed that flash of pain in Cassidy's beautiful green eyes and he'd gone a little crazy.

He'd shoved her up against her car and sucked her breath from her lungs and then she'd cried. The memory of her white, shocked face still had the power to make him feel like the worst kind of monster.

"Uh-huh," Ruben said mockingly.

He loved her, *dammit*. More than being a SEAL. More than his miserable life. More than he wanted to draw his next breath. And she'd told him to stop and had then fled as though she couldn't stand the sight of him.

"Nothing," he repeated wearily, shoving his hands through his hair and propping his elbows on the bar. He'd messed up and now he didn't know how to fix it.

"So," Ruben said, absently stirring his coffee, "this has nothing to do with a certain doctor you were seen practically inhaling whole in Bernie's parking lot, then?" Sam turned to glare at his brother. Ruben's sigh was as weary and heartfelt as Sam's had been a minute ago. "You're an idiot," Ruben said.

Sam straightened and opened his mouth to ream his sibling a new one, then shut it with a snap and looked away. No use denying it. He *was* an idiot.

"I messed up," he confessed roughly, swallowing past the lump of misery stuck in his throat like a burning lump of self-loathing.

"So fix it," Ruben said, his voice laced with steel and something that sounded like impatience-laced sympathy.

"Don't know if I can," Sam admitted quietly, shoving a shaking hand through his hair. "She hates me."

Ruben made a sound of irritation. "You're an embarrassment to Irishmen everywhere, you know that, Kellan?" he snapped, and when Sam's gaze flew up he added, "And here I thought your SEAL motto was 'Adapt and Overcome.'" He pointed a finger at Sam. "So get over yourself, and go do some adapting and overcoming."

"She doesn't want anything to do with me."

"You're a SEAL," Ruben reminded him ruthlessly. "Go be a SEAL. No obstacle too big and all that."

For long tense seconds Sam glared at his brother. He finally gave a sharp nod and downed the last of the god-awful coffee. He slapped the cup back in its saucer and shoved away from the bar.

"Pay the man," he ordered, before turning towards the door. "I've got something to do."

Groveling sounded about right, he admitted with a grimace. *And when I'm finished she's going to know she's mine—and that I'm hers.*

Failure was not an option. Not this time.

CHAPTER THIRTEEN

CASSIDY PUSHED OPEN the glass door to the sheriff's department, recalling the last time she'd been there. And like that night, Hazel Porter was once again manning the front desk.

The deputy peered over her half-spectacles and an odd expression crossed her face. She cleared her throat loudly once, then again, and abrupt silence fell over the room as a dozen pairs of eyes swung in her direction.

Forehead wrinkling in confusion, Cassidy approached the desk, suddenly feeling as nervous as a newlywed outside the honeymoon suite.

"Evening, Mrs. Porter," she greeted the deputy. "Dispatch said you…um…had a medical emergency?"

"Glad you could make it, hon," Hazel rasped, and turned to snag a bunch of keys from the board behind her. "We have a…situation."

"A situation?"

Hazel headed around the counter and made shooing gestures at the group of young deputies watching Cassidy with big toothy grins.

Cassidy frowned. "What's going on?"

Hazel shook her head. "Ignore 'em, hon, they're just a bunch of idiots with nothing better to do than stand around grinning like loons." The last she said loudly, scowling at the deputies who instantly tried to pretend they were busy.

Cassidy opened her mouth but the desk sergeant barreled on. "It's been a real slow week and nobody in this town can keep their noses out of other people's business."

Brow wrinkling with concern, Cassidy asked, "Are you all right, Mrs. Porter? You seem a little—"

"Call me Hazel, hon," the deputy interrupted, "everybody does. And I'm fine." Then she muttered something that sounded like, "Or I will be once all the hoo-hah is over," leaving a clueless Cassidy to follow her down the hallway towards the holding cells.

Muffled laughter and scuffling sounded somewhere behind her and she glanced over her shoulder. Several deputies were pushing and shoving each other to peer around the door—like they were in junior high.

They grinned and gave her the universal thumbs-up sign. *Weird,* she thought with a mental eye-roll, and turned back to follow Hazel's diminutive figure.

"This way, hon," the deputy said, unlocking the door and gesturing as if they hadn't done something similar a few months earlier. Stepping cautiously through the open doorway, Cassidy paused, wondering why every hair on her body was standing on end like a freaked-out cat.

Biting her lip uncertainly, she looked at the deputy and found Hazel staring at her with the oddest expression in her dark eyes.

"Don't be too hard on him, hon," Hazel murmured softly. "He's an idiot, but we love him."

Alarmed, Cassidy opened her mouth, certain now that Crescent Lake's sheriff's department was under some kind of Rocky Mountain madness. "Mrs. Porter—"

"It's Hazel, hon," the deputy interrupted cheerfully, and gestured to the large lump occupying the narrow bunk—in the same cell she'd entered before. "Now, in you go, everything's already set up. Holler if you need anything."

Squaring her shoulders, Cassidy stepped into the dimly lit holding area, vaguely aware that the cell doors were all ajar—and empty. *That's odd.* The outer door slammed shut.

She gave a startled squeak and told herself she was letting everyone's *weirdness* affect her.

Inhaling an unsteady breath, Cassidy tightened her grip on her medical bag and headed for the occupied cell. Stepping through the open doorway, she sensed movement behind her and whirled, using the momentum to swing her medical bag at the intruder. With a surprised curse, he ducked and lifted his forearm in a lightning-fast move that caught her wrist and sent the bag flying.

Squeaking in alarm, Cassidy scrambled backwards and stumbled over her own feet. She fell, landing hard, and for just a moment saw stars. Gasping for the breath that had been knocked out of her, she blinked and realized a man—*God, he was huge*—was bending over her...reaching for her.

She saw his mouth move but heard nothing over the blood thundering in her ears as she scuttled out of reach. But his big hands closed over her shoulders and before she could squeak out a protest, he'd hauled to her feet like she weighed nothing.

Intent only on preventing every woman's worst nightmare, Cassidy lashed out with her hands and feet, unaware that she was screaming until she heard a familiar voice calling her name.

"*Jeez*, Cassidy, stop. Stop it. *Cassidy!* Dammit. *Calm down!*"

She froze, gulping in great big sobs and stared into the dark face above her. It took her a couple of seconds to recognize the familiar masculine scent, the wide gold eyes staring at her as if she'd lost her mind.

She croaked, "*Samuel?*" and her knees abruptly buckled. He yanked her against his big warm body, hard arms keeping her from sliding to the floor.

"*Jeez*, woman," he growled into her hair, his arm an iron band across her back as she fisted her hands in his shirt and pressed her face into his warm throat. Her heart raced at warp speed. His free hand cupped the back of her head and she breathed in the comforting scent of heat, clean male and crisp mountain air.

By the time her heart dropped from stroke level to a mere freaked out, Cassidy remembered that she was furious with him—hell, he'd just scared a decade off her life.

Acting on impulse that was triggered by fear, fury and relief, she shoved him back and rammed her knee into his groin in one smooth move. With a startled yelp, he jerked away from the unexpected attack and dropped like a stone. Suddenly free, Cassidy hastily backed up until the cold steel bars bit into her shoulders.

"*Holy...*" Sam wheezed after a couple minutes of gasping like she'd gutted him with a scalpel. "*What...the...hell... was...that...for?*"

Shocked by her own action, Cassidy could only gape at him and stutter. "You... I... *Dammit!*" Her knees gave out and she slid down until her butt hit the cold floor. When her vision finally cleared and she could speak without stuttering, she opened her mouth to apologize and "You scared the *crap* out of me, you...you *dufus*!" emerged instead.

Sam stilled for a long moment then a rough sound emerged from his throat, sounding like a mix between a laugh and a groan. Moving slowly like he was in severe pain, he sat up and sank back against the bunk, one leg drawn up tightly to his chest. In the dim light his mouth was a tight white line in his green complexion.

Appalled by what she'd done, Cassidy rose on shaky legs, took a couple of wobbly steps and dropped to her knees beside him.

"I'm...I'm sorry," she gulped, lifting a hand to brush an errant lock of dark hair off his forehead. For a moment she enjoyed the feel of cool, silky strands between her fingers before admitting shakily, "I don't know why I did that."

His rough, gravelly laugh was abruptly cut off as he sucked in an unsteady breath and wiped his face with shaking hands. After a long silence he finally opened his eyes and stared at her.

"Dufus?"

She blinked. "What?"

"You called me a dufus."

Cassidy grimaced and sat back on her heels. "Yes… well…um. It was the best I could come up with in the heat of the moment."

His mouth curled into crooked smile and the expression in his eyes made her gasp. Before she could even begin to interpret it he said, "Come 'ere," and wrapped his fingers around her wrist.

With a gentle tug he pulled her towards him. She gave a startled squeak and found herself in his lap. His arms, his warmth, his scent surrounded her and she was tempted to wrap herself around him too. Just to prove to herself that he was here. Fortunately, she recalled his behavior of the previous night and pushed away. Sam tightened his arms with a deep, rough sound of pain.

"Don't…move," he rasped in her ear. "Just…gimme… a minute."

Realizing her bottom was planted right where she'd kneed him, Cassidy froze until she remembered that she was supposed to be treating an injured prisoner. *Him?*

"Where are you hurt?" she asked quietly, resisting the urge to run her hands, her lips over every inch of him.

He stilled and there was a moment of stunned silence. Then he lifted his head to gape at her. "*Really?* You do *that* and then ask where I hurt?"

A scalding blush rose into her cheeks and she bit back a hysterical giggle. "I'm s-sorry," she said in an unsteady voice. "But you deserved it for scaring me."

His snort told her what he thought of her apology. "I'll be lucky if you haven't permanently destroyed any chance I have of fathering future Kellans."

Reminded that he wasn't interested in making those

future Kellans with her, Cassidy snapped, "That's not my problem," and tried to scramble away. He yanked her back.

"Stop that," he ordered, clamping his hands on her hips and pulling her closer. "It *is* your problem." And then he murmured something that sounded like, "Or it will be…I hope."

Confused, Cassidy pulled back to look into his face. His color had returned but he still looked a little worse for wear.

"What's going on, Sam?" she demanded, lifting her hands to examine the bruises on his face, before probing his shoulders and chest. "The dispatcher called for a medic."

"Who just about crippled me. What's with the ninja attack, by the way?"

"Sam…"

He sighed. "Look, you're right I am a dufus. In fact—" *"Sam."*

"Just let me finish, okay," he interrupted quickly, his hands clenching on her thighs and sending little shivers of heat and arousal through her. "I need to say this."

Sighing, Cassidy studied him closely for signs of PTSD or at least an answer to his behavior. "All right," she said quietly, ruthlessly squelching the urge to squirm against him. "I'm listening, especially to the part where I'm right."

His mouth quirked up at the corner then tightened as he exhaled heavily. He looked nervous but Cassidy dismissed it as her imagination. He was a SEAL. The notion that he might be nervous made her want to smile. He'd survived being captured and tortured, for goodness' sake. Samuel J. Kellan didn't do nervous as much if not more than he didn't do relationships.

But something was clearly up and it was starting to make *her* nervous. "What are you doing here?" she asked quietly when the silence finally became unbearable. "Aren't you supposed to be parachuting into hostile territory and wiping out bad guys?"

"I quit," he said quietly, his gaze intense and unreadable on hers.

She blinked. "You…you…*what*? But…wh-why?"

He was silent for so long she didn't think he intended to reply but his gaze turned fiercely possessive when he finally admitted, "*You.*"

"Me. *Me?*" Her voice emerged as a squeak. "*What do you mean, me?*"

Sam's mouth lifted at one corner but his eyes were serious. "I mean I was on a mission and all I could think about was you. That's dangerous, Cassidy. For me *and* the team."

This close, Cassidy could see the individual muscles in his throat as he swallowed. Not knowing where to put her hands, she smoothed them down her thighs to disguise the fact that they were trembling.

"I messed up," he admitted softly. "I was five miles above the earth in a HALO jump and closing fast when my chute failed to deploy—"

Her head went abruptly light. "*Oh, my God*," she gasped out, clutching at his shoulders and shaking him. "Tell me…" she demanded hoarsely. "Tell me you're okay." His hands reached up to grab hers before she ripped his shirt.

"*Hey.*" His grip tightened. "I'm here, aren't I?"

She stared at him wide-eyed for a couple beats then pulled a hand free and punched him—hard. "*Dammit*, don't…don't you *dare* scare me like that."

He winced and wrapped long fingers around her wrist. "If you'll just let me finish," he said gently.

Cassidy swallowed a sob and grimaced. "Sorry."

He absently lifted her hand to plant a kiss on her white knuckles in a move that stunned her. "Well, there I was," he continued, "falling at a hundred miles per hour…" Her gasp earned her a chiding look. "As I said, a hundred miles per hour, with the earth rushing up to meet me, and I thought, This is it. I even relaxed, thinking it was nothing more than I deserved for failing my team." He paused and drew in a shaky breath. "Failing you. I heard someone yelling in my head and...*hell*...I was all ready to go out in a blaze of glory. Arm the grenades and aim for the target instead of the drop site...just blow everything to hell and back."

"*Oh, God, Sam no*," Cassidy cried out, slapping a hand over her mouth to hold in the ragged sound of shock and horror. Her eyes burnt with unshed tears and he tugged her close, smoothing a shaking hand over her messy ponytail to her back. "I was reaching for my stash, voices yelling in my ears, and the next second..." He pushed her away to look into her eyes. "The next second everything faded—like I'd blacked out—and I...I heard you...yelling at me to get my butt into gear." He paused and swallowed. "Then you said...*I love you Samuel, please*...please *don't go.*"

Stunned, Cassidy jerked back, fighting to free herself from his hold, but Sam's grip tightened, banding around her like steel, as though he couldn't bear to let her go. "*Don't*," he said hoarsely. "Don't pull away. I know I deserve it, but...just let me finish. *Please?*" He waited until she stilled, her face buried against his wide shoulder, tears dampening the soft, warm cotton.

"I saw your face, Cassidy," he said tightly against her temple. "As clear and real as you are to me now. And in that instant I knew... *Jeez.* You're right, I am a dufus. It took almost dying to realize that I...that I..." He halted and sucked in a sharp breath.

Cassidy froze and when he continued to breathe heavily she pushed away from him and lifted her gaze past the muscle twitching in his jaw. "That you what, Sam?"

His mouth twisted into a half-smile but his eyes glowed with an emotion Cassidy was too afraid to interpret.

"I was on a collision course with disaster. I blamed myself for living when my friends died. And when my chute failed I thought, *It's nothing more than you deserve.* But you rescued me, Doc, and even though I hurt you...didn't *deserve* you...I suddenly couldn't bear the thought of never seeing you again. That I hadn't told you." He inhaled shakily. "My mind was suddenly clear, like I was finally seeing the world for the first time. I sent up a prayer and yanked that damn clip.

"For a couple seconds nothing happened…and then… and then it deployed." He gave a ragged laugh and lifted his hands to cup her face. "Other than seeing your beautiful smile," he told her softly, "it was the most welcome sight I've ever seen."

"*Oh,*" was all Cassidy could manage, her voice low and raw.

"I love you Cassidy," he said solemnly. "Tell me it's not too late. Tell me I didn't dream those words. Tell me you didn't rescue me…my heart…only to break it."

"Oh, *Sam,*" Cassidy said again, too overwhelmed to think past the jumble of emotions rioting through her. "You're…sure?"

"That I love you? Dead sure—"

"*Don't say that,*" she burst out, placing a hand over his mouth. He paled, looking appalled. "Don't say that I love you?"

She let out a little giggle. "No," she said, smiling, leaning in to replace her hand with her mouth in a soft, sweet kiss. "You can say *that* as often as you like. In fact, you need to say it again."

Inhaling shakily, he thrust his fingers into her hair, his gaze falling to her mouth. "I love you," he groaned, his lips dropping to brush against hers. "God, you have no idea how much I love you."

Dizzy with happiness and wanting nothing more than to sink into his kiss, she throatily ordered, "Kiss me, then." But he pulled back, grinning at her growl of frustration.

He shook his head. "Not until you tell me."

"Tell you what?" she demanded huskily, leaning forward to catch his sculpted bottom lip between her teeth. She gave it a punishing nip and wriggled her bottom against him.

God, she'd missed this. His scent, his touch and the taste of him in her mouth.

"Aw, c'mon, babe," he groaned, pulling back to scowl at her. "Don't keep me in suspense."

Her mouth dropped open. *"Babe?"*

He gave her a hard shake. *"Dammit*, Cassidy," he growled. "I'm dying here. Rescue me, Doc...*please*."

Palming his tense face, Cassidy stared into his deep gold eyes, all humor abruptly disappearing. "I love you, Samuel Kellan," she murmured, her eyes soft on his before she caught at his mouth, and clung, like she'd never let go. "Don't you know? Don't you *know* yet how much I love you?"

A beautiful smile bloomed across his dark face and the next thing Cassidy found herself lying flat with his body, huge and heavy, pressing her into the cold floor. And before she could squeak out a protest, he slid a hand up her thigh to cup her bottom and pull her against him.

She thought he murmured, *"Thank God,"* and the next thing his mouth opened over hers in a kiss so hot and wet and *hungry* she nearly combusted.

Clutching at him, she sent her hands racing over his wide shoulders and back, down his arms, reveling in the solid feel of him beneath her palms. Her eyes drifted closed in delight and she gave herself over to his hunger.

For long moments Sam's mouth ravished hers as though he was starving for the taste of her, like he'd gone years instead of just weeks without her. She hummed her own hunger deep in her throat and marveled at the lights exploding behind her eyelids.

By the time they came up for air, she was gasping, dizzy with a pleasure she'd found only with him, and frustrated that they were still fully dressed. More than anything she wanted to feel the heated slide of skin against damp skin.

It was a few moments before she was able to open her eyes, only to discover a circle of curious, grinning faces peering down at them. Clutching Sam, she gave a startled squeak and felt her eyes widen as she recognized the young deputies who'd given her the thumbs-up earlier. Then the sheriff's face appeared overhead and then another...Sam's *sister?*

Oh, my God.

A hot blush rose in her cheeks. "*Sam,*" she squeaked, ducking her face into his throat.

"Yeah," he said in her hair, his voice strangely tight. "I know."

"Do you two need a room?" Hannah Kellan asked mildly, and laughter burst around them.

Sam stiffened, finally realizing they weren't alone. "What we need," Sam growled dryly, "is some privacy."

A moment later he rolled off Cassidy and drew her to her feet in one smooth move. He yanked her back when she made a move to bolt and tucked her against his side. He shook his head at their captive audience.

Hannah propped her shoulder against the open doorway and folded her arms beneath her breasts. "Well?" she asked cheekily, her elegant dark brow lifted in a way Cassidy recognized as pure Sam.

"Well, what?" he demanded, clearly annoyed by the interruption.

"Did she or didn't she?" Ruben demanded impatiently, and Cassidy nearly giggled at the way everyone's gaze jumped from one person to another in a ridiculous parody of a tennis match.

"I haven't asked her yet."

Hannah snickered and to Cassidy's embarrassment said, "What, too busy shoving your tongue down her throat?"

Sam growled threateningly and everyone laughed. "I'll be shoving you all out the door if you don't give us some space," he told her. "*Jeez*, can't a guy propose without the whole damn zoo turning up?"

Cassidy's head whipped up. "P-propose?" she squeaked.

His gaze turned possessive but to Cassidy's amazement he flushed. "Of course. What did you think I meant?" he demanded with a scowl.

"Well...I—"

His voice dropped. "You rescued me, Cassidy. You saved me when I didn't realize until it was almost too late. I love you. You're everything I want, everything I didn't realize I was looking for."

Cassidy's eyes misted and the buzzing in her ears almost blocked out the snickers of "*Aaaaww, isn't that sweet?*" coming from Sam's siblings.

"But...but what about your job?"

"I told you I quit."

"I don't know," she said slowly, ignoring the sharply inhaled breaths around them.

Sam froze and panic flashed across his face. "What do you mean, you don't know?"

"You haven't asked me yet," she reminded him gently, and reached up to kiss the corner of his mouth when he gusted out a relieved breath.

Turning her in his arms, he wrapped a hand around her neck and pressed his thumb beneath her chin, lifting her face to his.

"Cassidy Maureen Mahoney, will you rescue me one last time?"

Tears filled her eyes and her breath hitched in her throat.

"Oh, Sam—"

"Will you marry me?" he continued in a voice deep and clear and filled with emotion. "And spend the next sixty years loving me as much as I love you? Will you raise a family with me here in Crescent Lake and work by my side at the hospital, keeping the nosy locals healthy? Especially people who don't know when the hell to take a hint."

Her breath hitched. "Oh," she sighed, staring up at him with damp eyes until he couldn't stand the suspense.

"Say something, babe," he whispered pleadingly. "You're making me look bad in front of everyone."

She giggled and a sudden hush fell as every ear strained for her answer. "Yes…" she whispered into the hushed silence, and wild emotion burst into Sam's eyes.

"Yes?"

"Yes," Cassidy said a little louder. "Yes, I'll marry you." And when he gave a whoop she put up a hand. "But…." He stilled, the panic on his face priceless. His mouth dropped open and there was a smattering of snickers. "But?" He looked suddenly nervous and wary. "But what? I have to give up a kidney? Done. My family? With pleasure."

Cassidy's mouth curled in a private smile. "I want to know all your secrets."

"All of them?" And when her eyes narrowed he said quickly, "They're yours."

"Great. Now, what's the J for?"

He blinked. "Huh?"

"In your name," she explained, curling her arms around his neck and burying her hands in his thick, silky hair. She watched as a slow, sexy smile bloomed. He leaned closer to whisper in her ear and Cassidy pulled back, wild color blossoming in her cheeks. "I don't think so." She giggled. Sam sighed then tried again and when he finally pulled back, he let his brow rise questioningly.

Cassidy rose on her toes to seal the promise with a kiss. "Samuel James Kellan, nothing would make me happier than being your wife."

A deafening cheer rose to fill Crescent Lake's jail cells. Sam ignored the loud congratulations and celebratory backslaps to wrap his arms around the woman who'd rescued him from a life of nightmares.

"I love you, Doc Honey. What do you say we find someplace more private?"

A smile lit her face with love and anticipation and she blushed adorably. "I know just the place, Major Hotstuff."

He grinned. "Lead the way *babe*."

And she took his hand.

* * * * *

Mills & Boon® Hardback

April 2014

ROMANCE

A D'Angelo Like No Other — Carole Mortimer
Seduced by the Sultan — Sharon Kendrick
When Christakos Meets His Match — Abby Green
The Purest of Diamonds? — Susan Stephens
Secrets of a Bollywood Marriage — Susanna Carr
What the Greek's Money Can't Buy — Maya Blake
The Last Prince of Dahaar — Tara Pammi
The Sicilian's Unexpected Duty — Michelle Smart
One Night with Her Ex — Lucy King
The Secret Ingredient — Nina Harrington
Her Soldier Protector — Soraya Lane
Stolen Kiss From a Prince — Teresa Carpenter
Behind the Film Star's Smile — Kate Hardy
The Return of Mrs Jones — Jessica Gilmore
Her Client from Hell — Louisa George
Flirting with the Forbidden — Joss Wood
The Last Temptation of Dr Dalton — Robin Gianna
Resisting Her Rebel Hero — Lucy Ryder

MEDICAL

200 Harley Street: Surgeon in a Tux — Carol Marinelli
200 Harley Street: Girl from the Red Carpet — Scarlet Wilson
Flirting with the Socialite Doc — Melanie Milburne
His Diamond Like No Other — Lucy Clark

0314GEN STD HB

Mills & Boon® Large Print
April 2014

ROMANCE

Defiant in the Desert	Sharon Kendrick
Not Just the Boss's Plaything	Caitlin Crews
Rumours on the Red Carpet	Carole Mortimer
The Change in Di Navarra's Plan	Lynn Raye Harris
The Prince She Never Knew	Kate Hewitt
His Ultimate Prize	Maya Blake
More than a Convenient Marriage?	Dani Collins
Second Chance with Her Soldier	Barbara Hannay
Snowed in with the Billionaire	Caroline Anderson
Christmas at the Castle	Marion Lennox
Beware of the Boss	Leah Ashton

HISTORICAL

Not Just a Wallflower	Carole Mortimer
Courted by the Captain	Anne Herries
Running from Scandal	Amanda McCabe
The Knight's Fugitive Lady	Meriel Fuller
Falling for the Highland Rogue	Ann Lethbridge

MEDICAL

Gold Coast Angels: A Doctor's Redemption	Marion Lennox
Gold Coast Angels: Two Tiny Heartbeats	Fiona McArthur
Christmas Magic in Heatherdale	Abigail Gordon
The Motherhood Mix-Up	Jennifer Taylor
The Secret Between Them	Lucy Clark
Craving Her Rough Diamond Doc	Amalie Berlin

Mills & Boon® Hardback
May 2014

ROMANCE

The Only Woman to Defy Him	Carol Marinelli
Secrets of a Ruthless Tycoon	Cathy Williams
Gambling with the Crown	Lynn Raye Harris
The Forbidden Touch of Sanguardo	Julia James
One Night to Risk it All	Maisey Yates
A Clash with Cannavaro	Elizabeth Power
The Truth About De Campo	Jennifer Hayward
Sheikh's Scandal	Lucy Monroe
Beach Bar Baby	Heidi Rice
Sex, Lies & Her Impossible Boss	Jennifer Rae
Lessons in Rule-Breaking	Christy McKellen
Twelve Hours of Temptation	Shoma Narayanan
Expecting the Prince's Baby	Rebecca Winters
The Millionaire's Homecoming	Cara Colter
The Heir of the Castle	Scarlet Wilson
Swept Away by the Tycoon	Barbara Wallace
Return of Dr Maguire	Judy Campbell
Heatherdale's Shy Nurse	Abigail Gordon

MEDICAL

200 Harley Street: The Proud Italian	Alison Roberts
200 Harley Street: American Surgeon in London	Lynne Marshall
A Mother's Secret	Scarlet Wilson
Saving His Little Miracle	Jennifer Taylor

0414GEN STD HB

ROMANCE

The Dimitrakos Proposition	Lynne Graham
His Temporary Mistress	Cathy Williams
A Man Without Mercy	Miranda Lee
The Flaw in His Diamond	Susan Stephens
Forged in the Desert Heat	Maisey Yates
The Tycoon's Delicious Distraction	Maggie Cox
A Deal with Benefits	Susanna Carr
Mr (Not Quite) Perfect	Jessica Hart
English Girl in New York	Scarlet Wilson
The Greek's Tiny Miracle	Rebecca Winters
The Final Falcon Says I Do	Lucy Gordon

HISTORICAL

From Ruin to Riches	Louise Allen
Protected by the Major	Anne Herries
Secrets of a Gentleman Escort	Bronwyn Scott
Unveiling Lady Clare	Carol Townend
A Marriage of Notoriety	Diane Gaston

MEDICAL

Gold Coast Angels: Bundle of Trouble	Fiona Lowe
Gold Coast Angels: How to Resist Temptation	Amy Andrews
Her Firefighter Under the Mistletoe	Scarlet Wilson
Snowbound with Dr Delectable	Susan Carlisle
Her Real Family Christmas	Kate Hardy
Christmas Eve Delivery	Connie Cox

0414 GEN STD LP

Discover more romance at

www.millsandboon.co.uk

- ❤ WIN great prizes in our exclusive competitions
- ❤ BUY new titles before they hit the shops
- ❤ BROWSE new books and REVIEW your favourites
- ❤ SAVE on new books with the Mills & Boon® Bookclub™
- ❤ DISCOVER new authors

PLUS, to chat about your favourite reads, get the latest news and find special offers:

 Find us on facebook.com/millsandboon

🕊 Follow us on twitter.com/millsandboonuk

❤ Sign up to our newsletter at millsandboon.co.uk